Katharina Durrani

EXPERIRI

Part 1: Sathorja

NOVEL

WINDSOR VERLAG
www.windsor-verlag.com

Publisher: Windsor Verlag
ISBN: 978-1-627844-02-4

Translation: Fritz Nordsieck – Translations Fritz
Proofreading: Jürgen Kemmerer
Cover photo: Katharina Durrani
© Nejron Photo - Fotolia.com
Cover design: Julia Evseeva
Layout: Julia Evseeva

THE AUTHOR

Katharina Durrani, born in 1971, did an apprenticeship in book selling after her high school graduation followed by a course in graphic design at the school of arts in Vienna. Since her early youth she has a passion for writing poems and stories. She loves to allow her imagination to run free creating new virtual worlds. She also paints using several different techniques emphasizing fantastic things with intense colors.
Katharina Durrani is happily married living with her husband and her four children in Lower Austria.

'Ina, come on, we have to go!' A woman was calling her five year old daughter. She looked around, harried, while the baby in her arm grouched; no wonder it was getting its first teeth.

Staring bewildered at her mother, the little reddish-blonde haired girl asked: 'Mom, where are we going? Why do we have to go away from here? Where's Dad?'

'He's already waiting in the car, darling. Just walk over to him.'

Ina unwillingly trotted past her mother pulling behind her multicolored trolley; in the other hand she held her favorite cuddly toy Fiona, a white, stalk-eyed, fat unicorn.

When the car drove off five minutes later, Ina looked back once more. The one family house with the flourishing garden disappeared behind the townhouses of the nearby residential area.

'Where are we going?' Ina insisted stubbornly. Tears rolled down her cheeks; somehow she knew that she'd never see her home again.

'To Grandma', her father sighed. 'You're going to stay there. Mom and Dad have things to do.'

'I don't want!'

'You'll have fun. You know, Grandma's always cooking your favorite food, and she's playing 'Uno' with you for hours.' said her mother and blew her nose in a handkerchief.

'Mom, when are you coming back?'

'We'll be back very soon.'

Elsa was unable to look into the girl's eyes; with loving care she patted the baby in her arm in order to calm it down.

A year later, Ina's parents and her little sister Theresa were officially declared dead. Their car had been found burnt out in a patch of forest, and there was no trace of its owners.

'You've tried to reach me yesterday. What do you want?' a cheerful voice asked in the mobile phone. 'Oh', a young woman on the other end of the line sighed, 'I just can't cope with it yet, Eva.'
'Cope with what?'
'Don't play dumb; you know exactly!' Ina replied.
'Oh yes, that damned separation. You got rid of that idiot and you should be happy about it. You're twenty, aren't you? The whole world stands open for you!'
An uncomfortable silence spread. Eva just heard the gasping breath of her friend; she knew that Ina was weeping.
'Ok, darling, I'm coming to you right away.'
'Thank you', Ina sighed.
She let herself plop onto one of the moving boxes and stared into the air. She would give away everything she had to see her grandmother again. She had died of heart failure almost a year ago.

This was not the only blow of fate; less than three weeks ago her boyfriend had left her, too. Without saying a word he had simply moved out. But Ina knew exactly that he had met a tarted-up chick from his office, even though she was a completely different type of woman. Ina was of petite stature, had dense, long, reddish-blonde hair, freckles, and green eyes. Her ex-boyfriend's new flame was the exact opposite of her in appearance as well as in character. She was neither timid nor humble…

Minutes later the doorbell rang and Eva dashed into the flat. 'Here I am, and you don't know the fantastic idea I've got!'
Ina wiped her face with a handkerchief and murmured tonelessly: 'No.'
'A touch more enthusiasm, if possible,' Eva grinned. 'We'll go on a marvelous bicycle tour to provide an opportunity for different thoughts.'
'But isn't it already too late?'
'It's summer, and there're still two hours left before sunset. Come on, Ina!'
Their sweaty tour led them uphill, downhill, on country roads, and unpaved paths, through a little forest, and uphill again.
'Eva, just wait a minute!' Ina gasped shedding the sweat from her forehead. 'Can't we take a shortcut? I can't go on any further and I don't want to.' She had got off her bike, standing beside it and looking at the summer landscape. She could barely see a castle ruin in the mist in front of a hill telling the story of past times. The sky was turning orange; the setting sun had just disappeared behind a mountain ridge.
Ina pushed her bicycle under a big cherry tree and leaned against its trunk. When she looked up, she saw that there still were a few ripe cherries high up in the treetop, where only the birds could reach them. A tepid breeze carried the fragrance of summer; it was really a joy.
'Ina, just a little more and then it's downhill all the way home.'
Ina didn't say a word. She gazed into the distance – she had spotted a pale little dot quickly increasing in size and intensity.
'What's that?' she asked with an anxious voice while she was pointing to a strange thing that was quickly moving towards them. Eva yelled, but Ina got on her bike and rushed downhill.

There was a bright flash followed by an unreal cold. Then a deep hum cut through the air. Seconds later it was all over.

'You can calm down now', whispered a voice in Ina's confused consciousness. She didn't dare to look up; speechless and shivering she was staring at a board garnered with sweetishly fragrant petals freely floating about a yard above the floor. The smell was enticing, but why wasn't that thing simply lying on a table beside her? Damn, what was going on here? Was it witching hour? The green light flooding the room was all too suitable.

'I'm Maris.' Ina's entire body was trembling. 'It's all right', the woman's voice whispered softly. 'You are new here and …'

Ina didn't catch the rest while incredulously looking at her interlocutor. That language – she was certain she had never heard let alone learned it. But she could understand every single word.

It was difficult to estimate Maris' age. She had golden blond, curly hair and almost no wrinkles in her face. Her look rested on Ina with kindness and patience.

'You'll get used to it. On Sathorja many things are different from your planet Earth.'

Sathorja? Ina felt cold, freezing cold. She could hardly breathe; everything in front of her eyes became blurry and fuzzy, and her blood was hissing in her ears.

'You have made a long journey. Sathorja is a planet in a double star system with two suns many light years away from the Earth.'

'What?' Ina was out of breath; this was a nightmare! Nevertheless she was feeling her body – feeling every single fiber of it. The surroundings looked horrendously real.

She could touch her bed and grasp the drinking containers floating in the air on her right.
The room itself was perfectly circular. Half of its walls were made from glass allowing an impressing view on a strange landscape. There were gently undulating hills on the horizon, dark green forests, and part of a marvelous opal blue lake. All this was familiar to Ina, but she had never seen such a gnarled tree like the one outside the window. The pink colored leaves, giant violet blossoms, and pear-shaped, yellow fruits did not fit into Ina's repertoire of plants. Was she in the jungle? Oh, my God! Was that a bird? An animal looking like a dinosaur settled down on a branch directly in front of her. It had just a few grey feathers on a dark, scaled skin, an edged beak, and black eyes. It was quite an ugly creature that didn't really fit in with the multi-colored tree. Ina's eyes wandered around in the high room; there were lots of devices whose purpose she presumably never would understand. Sometimes glaring blue signs appeared projected in the air, changed, and then disappeared. Cautiously Ina tried to get up on her feet, but instantly a strong hand pushed her back onto the bed. 'Remain lying!' a deep voice exhorted. 'The coming days you'll stay here and follow my instructions.' Ina hadn't seen the man before and stared at him terrified. His grey eyes cold as ice gazed at her, and his hand rested on her chest. 'Do we understand each other?' Ina didn't even dare to nod. 'Silly thing', he wheezed. 'People reply to questions. So did you understand?' He looked down on her with a menacing expression.
'Let her alone, Ronok. Of course she heard you. The language decoder is functioning faultlessly', his wife Maris said.
'I have doubts with regard to Ina. We should have used better software than the conventional implants.'
Ina couldn't look away from the unequal couple. All the quick words didn't penetrate her mind; to her they sounded like a melody.

'What do you mean?' Maris asked her husband astonished. 'She's a difficult case', he answered. 'She's coming from the planet Earth, and you know exactly what that means. Look at her! She doesn't look very bright.'
'How would you feel, if you suddenly woke up in a completely crazy world after weeks of sleeping period? Ina is afraid and confused', Maris sighed.
'Do you think we did something wrong?' Ronok asked after a long break. Maris turned away.
Ina was moving around in her dream world. She imagined she was back on earth under the cherry tree leaning her bicycle against the smooth trunk. Eva?
'Eva!' she croaked with a dry throat. 'Where...is...she?'
Maris looked at her with surprise. 'Do you mean that black haired young woman who had been together with you?'
Ina nodded. What had they done to her? Had she also landed on this planet?
'She's all right', Maris replied haltingly. 'Where...' Ina began.
'We couldn't take her with us.'
'What?' Instantly Ina's eyes filled up with tears.
'She's on earth. She thinks you've gone on a journey.'
Eva. How many times had she phoned her friend, asking her for advice? They had done so many things together. What would she do now without her?'
'I'll never see her again, right?' Ina said in a wheezy voice.
Maris did not reply.
Ina was deeply shaken. She was all alone on a strange world. Eva would have known what to do. She always had the solution to every problem and was optimistic, quite unlike Ina. She wished to stand up and run out of this damned room in order to find a way home. At the slightest opportunity, no matter what it was, she would leave this planet!

'Is it her?' An about sixteen year old girl dashed into the laboratory where Ina was and looked at her for several seconds. Tears gathered in her eyes and began to run down her cheeks. She wiped them off with the back of her hand before she whispered: 'Welcome!'

'I'm Sesa', the girl went on softly. 'My parents have no time to welcome you, but they'll do so later on. Their names are Xio and Bora. My father is the president of the United Federation of Planets.' Sesa paused and took a deep breath.

'You are on Sathorja, a heavenly body similar to the planet Earth where you come from. Sathorja has two suns. It's a little smaller than your planet Earth, the circadian rhythm is different, and so are the weeks, months, and years. Of course, fauna and flora are different from your home planet, but human beings are also living here like on your planet. However, our civilization is peaceful and more advanced than yours. We have no wars. Machines are doing most of the work, but you already know that from your home planet.' She seemed to practice these sentences a lot; she rattled them off quickly and sometimes a little vague.

'Sesa, speak a bit slower', Maris remarked softly. 'Ina cannot even follow you.'

'Oh well, I'm very sorry about that experiment. We haven't been able to prevent that. Ronok, our doctor, insisted in performing it', Sesa went on unperturbed. The girl swept with her hands over her rosy cheeks again, her eyes became glassy, and her pretty face looked sad. She

had elaborately pinned up her brunette hair and decorated it with glittering stones. Her floor-length, green shimmering gown was hanging formlessly on her body concealing her delicate figure. Sesa wasn't very self-confident, her gaze traveled constantly into the distance – she didn't dare to look into Ina's eyes. Ina, however, was baffled staring at Sesa. She felt an inexplicable intimacy.
'You know, Ina', Sesa sniveled all of a sudden; 'it was my idea to bring you here. I didn't bear in mind that you have absolutely no rights here. Well…' she got stuck for a moment looking for the right words. 'From now on you will have to live with gills. I'm very sorry', she said with a sob. Ina swallowed looking at Sesa as if she was out of her mind. Then she looked at Maris who was still standing in front of her bed.
'That's true', Maris murmured.
Ina felt as if she couldn't breathe. Everything became blurred in front of her eyes while she was desperately gasping for breath. Less than a minute later Ina fell into deep and peaceful sleep. The soporific Maris had given her was known as very effective.

'Ina went nuts when Sesa told her about the experiment. It'll take a long time until she gets used to the fact of having gills. Nobody knows how much time remains for our daughter Shora.' Maris looked at her husband with great concern. 'I'm very afraid and I can't help to think we have done terribly wrong to Ina.'
'Nonsense, Maris', Ronok replied. 'First of all, she belongs to an inferior species; therefore it's senseless to say we are doing her wrong. Secondly, I hope you haven't forgotten what happened fifteen years ago, and who was to blame for it.'
'But it wasn't Ina, darling. Sometimes I think you just want to take revenge for the terrible things that happened in those days. You've just waited for the right moment because you haven't been able to forgive them all

these years. Ina just came in handy!'
'You're crazy' Ronok replied angrily. 'You know exactly that there's no other way to save our daughter. All the diving robots broke down, and we have no financial resources anymore.'
'But…' Maris sighed.
'I have been able to get sponsors for the experiment, but not for robots! And even that was difficult.'
'Just tell me one thing: Would you have used Ina for the experiment, if she hadn't been badly hurt in that accident?'
'Of course I wouldn't. That was our chance.'
In this very moment a very old and stooped woman shuffled towards them. She had short, snow-white hair, and her face was full of wrinkles suggesting a lot of wisdom. Her vivid eyes were looking at Maris. 'Don't worry, love', she said with a brittle voice. 'At the moment Shora is stable. I have enough supplies of medicinal fruits; so take it easy. Ina will take several weeks until she can dive and get Gaia-fruits.'
'Hallo Liess!' Maris cried out happily hurrying towards the old Sathorjan woman to lead her to an armchair.
Liess was an exceptionally gifted healer and herbalist and knew a medicinal plant for any ache and pain. Sathorja's biodiversity was rated as legendary both in fauna and flora, on land and in the water. They were able to supply the entire Federation of Planets with raw materials for numerous medicaments. Several factories produced and distributed pharmaceuticals. Especially fruits from certain water plants from the Loki Lake were in great demand. They only grew in a deep rift in complete darkness. The warm currents there offered good growing conditions for these rare plants.

'I cooked up a tonic to invigorate our guest and I thought I better come to bring it personally', Liess said winking at Maris. 'Thank you', Maris murmured surprised.

'Oh, well, that's wonderful', the old woman remarked while she was scrutinizing Ina. 'The little one is already looking much more vigorous. Thanks to her young age she's recovering really quickly.'
'That's right', Maris said with a loud sigh. 'But she has serious problems to understand all this.' She felt her eyes wetting when she thought of her daughter. Again she was afraid to lose her daughter. She'd been such a lively girl; five years ago she had married and given her two granddaughters. Then she suddenly got ill. She couldn't eat anymore, got weaker and weaker, her skin turned as white as a sheet, and she had periodic bouts of fever. Maris and her husband had travelled to visit her, and they had consulted experts of various nations, but all in vain. Nobody knew what was wrong with her. Until the day she met a woman, a Koni. She had the ability to track down diseases. Her diagnose was shattering. Shora had only a short time left to live. Maris' gaze wandered over to the sleeping earthling. Ina was Shora's last and only hope. But all this was quite absurd. How could this creature overcome the dangerous currents in the lake, where technology had failed? How could she accomplish to dive in total darkness to get these fruits in a place, where hot water was sputtering out of pits in the rock?
Ronok and Maris had thought of everything. Ina was able to dive up to 100 feet deep. Her eyes and skin were adapted to the life under water. Of course there still were a couple of unresolved problems as for example the annoying buoyancy of the human body. Ina was a human being and would always be just that.
Maris let her head sink into her hands.
'I know that you are torn between your hopes and doubts, but Ina will do it', the old lady said convinced.
'Well, I really have my doubts', Ronok sighed. 'She comes from the planet Earth and…'
'Why do you complain? Didn't you choose Ina yourself for the experiment?'

'I had no choice, Liess.'

'What difference does her planet of origin make?' the old lady asked. 'Ina has a good heart, my love.'

'How do you know?' Ronok said and cast an angry glance at the herbalist.

'I can feel it. Ina will help you. But remember, she's a sensitive, fragile human being, and even more after that intervention.'

'That's all right, Liess', Ronok said with a shake of his head.

Oh no! Ina sat up with dismay. Her gaze wandered over the floating devices stacked on top of each other. She still was lying in that same nightmarish room. The green diffuse light made the room look eerie. Maybe all this was just a bad dream. Sathorja? Who had created this world? Had it been God?
She rejected this idea and turned to the window front. What time could it be? Outside dawn was beginning to break. To the right a phosphorescent moon was reflected on a water surface. Ina stretched to be able to see more. The major part of the lake was concealed by the dense foliage of the trees. The branches stood out black against the awaking landscape causing an eerie impression. Something was moving in the tree top, but Ina couldn't see what it was. A slight shudder came over her. The sunrise of the twin suns distracted her. How was this possible? Two suns like orange red balls rose behind the branches moving gradually upward.

Cautiously she swung her legs out of the bed and stood up. Desperately fighting against the arising vertigo, she began to waver and fell down. But what was happening? She had expected a hard impact, but she fell smoothly. The floor yielded under her weight and felt warm to the touch. And that wasn't all: a mild green light began to shine underneath her body. Ina sat up. Her surroundings wavered dangerously, and nausea joined vertigo.
'Ina!' Maris rushed to help the earthling. 'What has happened?'

Ina turned around. 'I just wanted to…' she stammered.
'What are you doing on the floor?' Ronok lifted her up with a brisk sweep of his hand and put her back onto the bed.
'Yesterday I told you to follow my instructions', he said ominously. 'Do you remember? Did I say something like getting up and walking around?'

Ina felt like a cornered animal. Scared and shivering she stared at the Sathorjan. Instinctively she had to think of her father although she couldn`t remember him very well. The men were very similar in age, build and shape. But the way Ronok looked at her was the complete opposite. His eyes were icy cold, and there was not the slightest sign of compassion or comprehension in them.
'Well, I'll try to talk to you on your level', the angry physician went on. 'You are too weak to get up yet.'
'Why?' Ina was surprised that she dared to ask. It seemed extremely strange to speak this melodic language.
'Since you have been sleeping for many weeks, your body has to get used gradually to normal life again. Do you understand this or are you too stupid?' After a short break he added: 'Furthermore, you are enfeebled by the experiment.'
Oh my God, thought Ina panicking, when she remembered the previous day. Gills? Why for heaven's sake should it be necessary to do this to a human being? She touched her neck with both hands and her cold, clammy fingers were looking for incisions.
'No, not there where everybody can see them', Maris explained who so far hadn't said a word. 'They are on each side under your arms. Like this they are protected between the ribs and can't be seen easily.'
'It's difficult, but it can be done', Ronok commented. 'Since the intervention, your lungs have less capacity. You should pay attention to this.'
Was that a dumb joke? Ina became alternatingly hot and

cold. She was staring at the couple with eyes and mouth wide open. Her mind rebelled. 'No!' she gasped again and again, until Maris finally achieved with Ronok's help to pour the soporific into her mouth.

'Look, darling! Ina is completely out of her mind. She cannot and doesn't want to accept it.'

'I know', said the doctor. 'I'm afraid it'll take some time.'

'I hope we'll have enough time. This morning Shora looked terrible. Her skin was transparent, her hair was brittle, and…' Maris swept the tears out of her eyes.

'Don't be afraid, darling. We must trust Liess.'

Sesa stared impatiently at the young woman. 'Wake up!' Softly she shook up Ina and pointed with an expansive gesture to a couple that was accompanying her. 'This is Xio, my father and Bora, my mother.' Ina rubbed the sleep from her eyes. Plenty of visitors! Couldn't they leave her alone to have some peace and quiet?

'It's nice that you finally came here, Ina.' Bora extended her hand. She had no resemblance to Sesa. She was chubby with a round white face without any wrinkles. Glaring red lips and the eyes encircled in blue. Her hair stood out in an unnatural bluish black. Her dress looked like a sack; it was neither fitted to her waist nor adorned. The clothing material was the same color and shimmered like Bora's hair.

'You like our fashion, don't you?' the Sathorjan woman asked rearranging her hairdo.

Ina just said: 'Hm.'

'How do you like it here?' Xio asked. Ina didn't know what to say and looked at Sesa seeking help.

'So far she hasn't seen more than the laboratory', Sesa commented deploring.

'This will soon change, love. Your apartment is waiting for you. It's equipped for your requirements.' Xio paused for a moment, then he said: 'Well, you probably want to know, why you're here on Sathorja.'

'Because of Sesa', Ina murmured.

'Don't you think that's strange?' Bora asked.

'Should I?'

Xio cleaned his throat and said: 'You have been selected to bring up precious raw material from the bottom of the lake.' Ina swallowed and looked at him as if he were nuts. 'Our medical care depends on the fruits of a rare water plant.'
I beg your pardon. Didn't they have machines doing the difficult jobs for them? Why exactly should she fetch these medical fruits? Was this the reason why she had gills?
'What…?' Ina stuttered confused.
'You have to start harvesting within the next couple of weeks; otherwise Ronok and Maris' daughter will die.'
Horrified Ina turned to Maris who had been listening without saying a word. She began to understand. Obviously she was predestined to save Shora. But Ina wasn't a hero at all; she was neither courageous nor strong. How could these lunatic Sathorjans think, she could accomplish something under the water in that lake?
'And there's more, Ina', Bora declared theatrically. 'We brought you from the planet Earth, because…' Ina turned pale. Was this still not enough?
'No, please, keep quiet!' hissed Maris. She hated that nobody listened to her. But the president's wife had decided to talk and Maris had no chance to keep her from doing so.
'Ina, Sesa is your little sister Theresa.'
For a long moment Ina stared at Bora. Then she let out a loud scream: 'You're lying!' She shut her ears and went on screaming.
'What have you done?' Maris groaned angrily.
'What's the problem?' Bora asked naively. 'It's just the pure truth.'
'Don't you understand that all this is just too much for her?' Maris was really annoyed now. Sorrowfully she looked at Ina who gave rein to her desperation and impotence.
Annoyed Xio shook his head. He shouldn't have granted his daughter's petition. Taking Ina here and away from Earth had been one of the greatest mistakes he had ever made…

Early the next morning Sesa rushed through the long and winding corridors to the laboratory. Her vehicle was floating silently about two feet above the ground, leaned into the curves and speeded through the large and mighty entrance hall of the castle. Sesa was sitting on the floating platform like Aladdin on his magic carpet. It was quiet, and there was nobody around. In one hour it would get busy here, but before that she had to help Ina to escape. She owed this to her after putting her into this mess.

She had to ask Alons, a young Sathorjan, for help. She hated it, but she had no choice. Only he could achieve that she could stay an hour with Ina without anyone's knowledge. Sesa took a brief look on the sparkling bracelet adorned with stones she wore on her wrist. Every citizen had to wear those damned CC3s in the castle. Her father insisted that everybody wore these unnecessary microcomputers. For years, the total surveillance had been very annoying for her. Constantly her parents asked her, why she was hanging around in boutiques instead of studying. Why should the security department always know where every individual was at any time of day? That was a real problem for her now. She had to find a way to get Ina unseen out of the laboratory. She wanted to bring her to the Loki Lake. From there, due to Ina's new abilities she would be able to dive to the next city, take a space shuttle, and travel back home to Earth. So far, so good.

She had told Alons a fairy tale, something about sisterly love and intimacy. That idiot had believed her and had reprogrammed her and Ina's CC3. Nobody would notice the disappearance of the terrestrial woman, if they only were quick enough.
'Ina, wake up!' Sesa shook her sister gently.
'What's going on?' Ina cast an angry look at Sesa. 'You dare to come here? After all what has happened?' Her voice was getting louder and nearly cracked.
'I…' Sesa began insecurely, but Ina grabbed her shoulders and shouted at her: 'Are you trying to be my friend?' For a moment she looked into the young Sathorjan's eyes discovering something painfully familiar. She took a deep breath and pushed Sesa away. 'Don't play with the feelings of other people! My sister Theresa is dead just like my parents.' Ina wiped the tears away from her cheeks and sighed: 'Get lost!'
Sesa didn't say a word; despair and sadness invaded her soul like a dark shadow. Time was running out; she had to take action, otherwise all the preparations would have been in vain.
'I want to help you to escape. I have planned every detail.' Sesa had turned away; she didn't dare to look at her sister. 'I know ways and means to bring you back to your home planet.'
'What are you talking about?' Ina pricked up her ears. Ineffable joy filled her heart; those words seemed to be a gift from the heavens, a miracle. She thought of what she would do once she was back to Earth. First of all she would look for Eva and rent a new flat. She'd buy a dog puppy against her loneliness and go back to her job. Well, there might be a little problem with the gills, but she didn't care. She'd go back home, and that was essential!
Ina was stunned. She stood up and joined Sesa.
'I'll bring you to the Loki Lake. From there you can swim to Rambala.'
'What's Rambala?'

'Rambala is a nearby city that has a space port. But first you have to cross a small portion of the lake to get away from here.'
'Do you want me to do so?'
'You have understood, Ina. I want you to dive.' Her sister was still looking perplexed, so Sesa said in a low voice: 'The experiment, you know.'
For a moment Ina put her hands under her arms.
'Does it hurt?' Sesa asked worried. Then her plan would be doomed to failure.
Ina shook her head. 'That can't be true', she said lost in thought.
'We have very little time left, Ina', she snatched Ina's wrist and had a look on the shimmering bracelet, Ina's CC3. 'Time is running out. Come on!'
'Why should I trust you?' Ina suddenly shouted and tore herself free.
'You should, because I am Theresa!' Sesa was losing her temper.
'That's impossible!' Ina nagged, 'How did you get here?'
'I came with our parents.'
'Are they alive?' Ina asked in a quivering voice. Memories lit up in front of her inner eye.
'Yes, but I don't know exactly where they are. They have been banned, and I have absolutely no contact with them.'
'For heaven's sake, how did you get to Sathorja?'
'We came in a space ship of the Sathorjan fleet. Our parents discovered it in a clearing in the forest and went aboard as stowaways.'
'Can you do that?' Ina asked. The story became more and more unbelievable.
'You know, the Sathorjans love to travel. Frequently missions to other solar systems are taking place. They have already been visiting the Earth several times. Our parents owed money to some crooks. They feared for their lives, and the unsecured space ship suited them well. Due to a

defect in the security system they have been able to come aboard the shuttle unnoticed', replied Sesa impatiently.
'I'm sure you can also tell me why they left me behind.' Ina noticed a burning rage in her heart.
'I don't know exactly. I was told that you had given us away. You haven't been in danger or something like this.' Enraged Ina stared at her sister.
'Unfortunately we were discovered. A huge turmoil erupted in the ship, an incredible chaos. But then it was already too late to return.'
'And how did it go on?'
'Our parents Chris and Elsa were anaesthetized and brought away. Since then I didn't see them anymore.'
'That means, you really don't know them', Ina deduced. 'And what did they do with you?'
'Oh, I was a sweet little baby. Bora fell in love with me at once and wished to keep me. She and Xio couldn't have children, so they adopted me in a fast track procedure. And Theresa became Sesa.' She looked at her bracelet again. There was only a short time left.
'Nonsense', Ina said shaking her head. 'This outrageous story cannot be true. You made it all up, didn't you?'
'No Ina, I didn't. Just recently I was told about your existence and I begged my adoptive parents to bring you to Sathorja. Come on now. If you want to leave the laboratory, we have to go now.'
'Can I change my clothes?' Ina asked angrily.
'No. Otherwise we won't make it to the lake anymore.' She looked at her bracelet again.
'Why do you constantly stare on that wristband? It's nice, but…'
'Ina', Sesa sighed unnerved. 'I'll explain it to you on the way, right?'
Ina nodded and followed her sister out of the lab. A transport robot was waiting in front of the door.
'What's that?' Ina asked horrified. It was a gently blinking floating platform with handgrips and seat pans.

'It's a transporter. Just sit down on it. Or do you want to go on dealing with our doctor?'
Certainly she didn't. Obediently Ina climbed onto the machine, quickly took her seat, and held on.
Suddenly and without previous warning the vehicle darted off, and Ina had to close her eyes. The bright light from the rising twin suns flooded the corridor made from glass, they were driving along. Ina's hands cramped up in each curve. Light and colors, glass and tiles, interior patios with mighty trees, steps, and large halls were passing by at a breathtaking speed.
'Tell me, how big is this building?' Ina asked amazed.
'It's huge. Our destination is the arrival hall. Right in front of us it's turning downward. Cling on tight!'
Actually the corridor they were following was widening, the tiled floor below them suddenly broke off, and Ina cried out loudly.
'We are about to arrive!' Sesa tried to calm down her sister. In steep curves the transporter spiraled down until it reached the floor of the hall. In a moderate height of about three feet the platform floated towards a huge, closed gate.
'Welcome at the Gon Hall!' Sesa said happily. They had arrived just on time. Due to the racy flight they had caught up a few minutes.
'Wow, that's enormous!' Ina acknowledged. The strange feeling in her stomach due to the quick descent was gradually disappearing.
Enchanted Ina contemplated the crystalline construction that was sparkling in the light of the rising suns.
'Incredible', she sighed blinking her eyes, 'that's very beautiful!'
'You think that's very beautiful, because you haven't seen the shopping promenades yet.'
Ina was soaking up the surroundings. She felt like in a fairy tale. Comfortable seats glittering in all colors were spread everywhere inviting to sit down. Flowering plants

all over the place made these oases more pleasant to live in order to distract from the daily stress. Stairways led from one level to the other; it was even possible to go up to the roof, if one wished.

All of a sudden the vehicle stopped. Ina banged her head painfully against Sesa's back. 'What's going on?' she asked and rubbed her face.
'I've been expecting you already.' A young Sathorjan stood directly in front of the transporter and stared angrily at Sesa.
'Farres, what's the point of that?' Sesa asked surprised. She knew the young man for years. He worked at the security department of the palace like his brother Alons. Both were known as true and faithful staff members although Alons had some extra income... However Farres strictly followed the current laws, was duteous and reserved. Sesa had already asked him several times, why he was together with that tarted girl Rida. They didn't have any common hobbies. Farres loved nature, did a lot of sport, and had a keen sense of justice. Lost in thoughts, Sesa shook her head.
'Do you really think my brother is stupid enough to provide your sister a chance to escape? Do you know the severity of penalty for such an offense?' –
'I'll take the responsibility for this. I'll never betray Alons or you, okay? Now step aside, please!' But the Sathorjan didn't move at all. Unnerved Sesa slid down from the transporter platform.
Yet Ina seemed to be petrified. She was looking overtly at the Sathorjan. When he turned his look to her, she suddenly blushed.
'Ina?' asked Sesa astonished. 'What's wrong with you? Have you never seen a man?'
Ina's face reddened even more. Quickly she turned to the transporter as if she was interested in the vehicle.

'Hallo, Ina!' Farres grinned amused by the terrestrial's behavior. For a moment, Ina lifted her head and looked deeply into the beautiful brown eyes of the young Sathorjan. Wow, this guy was incredibly attractive: His dark complexion, black hair, and athletic, slender figure!
'Are you all right?' he asked.
She wasn't really; not one word passed over her lips.
Sesa seized the opportunity. The air was filled with tension between Ina and Farres, and Sesa had to take advantage of the momentaneous confusion. She jumped on the transporter and started it with a tiny movement of her hand. The platform quickly went backwards and then rose more than ten feet high, while Ina anxiously clung to the handgrips. High up in the air, the vehicle whizzed through the hall. Farres cast a curse and rushed behind the two girls, but shortly after he had to abandon the race. The sisters were already out of range.
The transporter headed straight for the entrance gate. Horrified, Ina cried out: 'We're going to die!', when she noticed that the gate slowly opened. Ina thought the gap was too small; she closed her eyes fearing a painful crash.
'We did it', Sesa sighed relieved, stopped the transporter and got off. 'Where are we?' Ina asked puzzled. She stood at the rim of a circular open space surrounded by dark blue, high trees. She turned around looking in all directions and discovered some multicolored tiled pathways leading away from the circular space.
'Later I'll explain it to you', Sesa said and grabbed Ina's arm leading her along an overgrown trail.
'Farres will follow us!'
Oh, really? Hmm, I wouldn't mind! She suddenly stopped and turned around. Where was the crystalline palace, the entire huge building? It couldn't have vanished in thin air, could it? Now they were all alone just surrounded by greenery and fantastic vegetation. Really strange; they hadn't seen anybody the whole morning.

'I'm not going any further', Ina complained staring at the place, where the castle should have been. 'Where did it go?'
'Ina, come on now! In a few minutes our time is running out, and you won't want that all our efforts have been in vain.' Sesa raked her fingers nervously through her hair.
'And then?'
'They'll give the alarm. They'll notice that you left the lab and look for you. Ronok will be very angry and…' These last words had an astonishing effect on Ina. She began to run and gasping she followed her sister. The fragrance of myriads of flowers befuddled her mind as did the memory of Farres. Who was that strange guy? She felt the need to stop and wait for him. A thorny branch scratched her arm.
'Ouch', hissed Ina.
'Pay attention! The trail is full of scrub.'
Ina continued to run, stumbled over a glaring red stone and almost fell. The undergrowth opened up. In front of the two women lay a huge lake of turquoise color. It was breathtaking. Ina had never seen such a beautiful panorama.
'That's fantastic', she cried out with excitement.
The water was as smooth as a mirror shimmering in the sunlight; flowering bushes lined the sandy shore. A marvelous sunbathing lawn extended to the right, filled with colorful weeds. Behind them Ina could recognize the skyline of a distant city. On the left there was nothing but water. The lake seemed endless.
'Magnificent!'
'You like it very much; that's nice, but you have no time to enjoy it. Now listen carefully: You swim in the direction of the suns, ok?'
'How far?' Ina asked. 'Up to a point you nearly lose sight of the shore.'
'Are you crazy? I'm not able to do that. Impossible!' Ina moaned shaking her head.

'Yes, you can', said Sesa determined. 'Then you turn towards the city. You can see it perfectly from the water; trust me. You'll recognize a high, luminous tower. When you reach the shore, a glider will come to pick you up and bring you to the airport. I have organized it all.' Sesa cast a proud look at her sister.
'What's a glider?'
'It's called like this, Ina. Look, there's one on the horizon!' Sesa pointed to a dark shadow just above the water moving at high speed. 'They are the most common means of transport here.'
'Everything must float here', Ina sighed shaking her head.
'Ok, I have packed a bag for you', Sesa held an unsuspicious traveling bag in her hand. Strange, Ina hadn't even noticed it before. 'It's waterproof. You can sling it over your shoulders, and it won't hinder you when you're swimming.'
'What do I need this for?' Ina asked disparagingly looking at the flat surface of the Loki Lake.
'You'll need a couple of things, Ina', said her sister stubbornly. 'There's a robe, Quados, and something to eat and to drink.'
'Does all this fit in there?' her sister asked amazed. She took the bag and then stopped again. 'What are Quados?'
'You have to use the Quados when you go ashore. You must always use them; otherwise you can't be in the open air.'
'What?' Ina screamed.
'It's like this and…'
'Sesa, Ina!' They could clearly hear Farres' voice.
Ina stopped and listened carefully. Did she really want to escape from Sathorja? She didn't get this man out of her mind. He had looked at her in a way, in a way…
'Hurry up!' Sesa was shifting nervously from one leg to the other looking at her bracelet. 'Your CC3 will be activated in less than ten minutes.'

'My what?'
'Your CC3. It's a microcomputer connected with the primary computer in the security department. You have to keep it under water. Like this you can cut the connection, you understand?'
'Can't we simply take that thing off?' asked Ina and slid her fingers over the bracelet. It was beautiful.
'No!' Sesa was all run down. Ina obviously didn't understand the seriousness of her situation.
'Take your clothes off; you must go into the water.'
'Naked?' asked Ina spontaneously.
'You are wearing swimwear under your robe', Sesa moaned. Hastily she helped her sister to take off her clothes. 'Let's go!' she shouted, shooing her sister into the cold water. 'Remember Ronok!' she yelled at her.
This name filled her with horror sending shivers down her spine. She waded courageously into the lake. She still heard Sesa shouting: 'Take the Quados off your gills!'

'That was not a good idea!' commented Farres, when he reached the shore. 'She doesn't have the slightest chance. I hope she'll be back in the lab in a short period of time.'
'Are you crazy? Don't you know what Ronok is doing to her?' Sesa replied angrily.
'Yes, I've heard about it. Anyway, this could be changed. But not the weather. Sesa, didn't you see the upcoming storm front in the west?' He pointed to the towering clouds appearing at the horizon.
'That's nonsense. It's not coming here.'
'Don't you feel the wind?'
'That doesn't matter. Ina just has to swim under water, and she'll be safe.'
'She is not familiar with the lake. I'll alert the security forces.'
'She'll never forgive you, Farres.'
'It'll save her life.'
'Do you seriously believe she wants to live like this?'

Farres turned away from Sesa and looked out on the Loki Lake. Ina just was a little dot far away. It looked as if she was afraid of diving…

Aghast Maris stood in the lab without knowing how to tell her husband about Ina's escape. A sharp warning sound made her shake: An alarm had been triggered.
'What's going on?' Ronok asked his wife looking at the empty bed. 'How could that happen?' Maris shrugged and shook her head. 'Sesa!' concluded Ronok, 'She is behind this.'
'But how could she have avoided the security mechanisms?' Maris looked at her husband doubtfully.
'Nothing is unlikely with that girl.'
'She might be able to do it, but where could Ina have been brought to?'
Ronok didn't say a word. Thoughtfully he looked out of the window. On the horizon one could see part of the Loki Lake. Was Ina there? Ronok rejected the idea and left the laboratory.

What was this? Was she dreaming?
Ina was just about four feet under the water surface staring into the deep blue of the lake. Just a moment; how was that possible? Was she dead? No, she was breathing; she could feel it. Ina began to kick wildly with her legs. When she turned around, she saw the sky above her and surfaced. She greedily soaked the mild breeze into her lungs. Damn, all around there was nothing but water. There was no land in sight, no matter the effort she made to see the shore on the horizon. Ina tried desperately to remember. Sesa, her sister, had helped her to escape and she had been swimming like hell. Eventually she had been floating at the surface to rest and actually she had fallen asleep. The current must have driven her away. Sesa's sophisticated plan had failed completely.
Ina thoughtfully watched the dark clouds towering up. They were rising up and beginning to cover up the suns. If she wasn't wrong, soon a heavy thunderstorm would rumble over the lake. She had to hurry up and quickly get away from here. Her entire body ached, when she began to move again. Frequently she had to take a rest lying flat on the water without moving. She looked at her upper part of the body. Damn, what was this? She had lots of incisions between the ribs. Stunned she slid her fingers over them secretly hoping she was dreaming. But she could clearly feel the touch! Oh no, the experiment! Did she really have gills?
'Why', she shouted against the upcoming storm. The answer came right off: A loud roll of thunder hurt her

ears. Torrential rain started to come down on her. The thunderstorm seemed to discharge directly above her. She was panicking and swam a little further. Then she followed her survival instinct and dived down into the Loki Lake.

'Why didn't you stop her?' Xio shouted at the young Sathorjan.
'Sesa has fooled me', Farres admitted sheepishly.
'And where is she now?' Losos, the chief of the security department, asked looking inquiringly at the president.
'Under house arrest in my apartment', Xio stated in an unaccented voice. 'She admitted everything. She wanted to help her sister.'
'Well, that went rather wrong.'
Nuna, a young staff member of the security department looked quite helplessly, while she was making a phone call. 'What shall I tell him?' she asked Losos distressed.
'Who are you talking to?' Losos asked impatiently.
'It's Ronok. He is very upset and wants to talk to you at once.' Losos nodded reluctantly and took the phone call over to his CC3. It was hard to believe that the ring on his little finger contained a highly intelligent microcomputer.
'Where is she?' shouted Ronok displeased.
'As I already told you, she's in the Loki Lake. Farres just confirmed it.'
'Are there any gliders looking for her?' the doctor asked after a short break.
'No.'
'What does that mean?'
'Didn't you see the thunderstorm outside?'
'I can only hope, Ina is staying on the bottom of the lake', Ronok panted with rage. 'As you know, the girl's essential for Shora's survival.'

Losos ended the call and noticed Xio's guilty look.
'My daughter didn't know what she was doing', he said quickly.
'As soon as the storm is over, we'll try to find Ina. But there's a little problem.'
'What is it?'
'CC3s don't function under water. In order to be located, Ina must be on the surface', explained Losos and looked worried.
'She's a human being, so her buoyancy will drive her up to the surface, when she...' Nuna stopped affected and looked back on the big hologram showing the Loki Lake. Bright dots marked the striking flashes.
Farres had gone back to his workplace, but instead of doing his job, he was looking out of the window. Ina, the girl from the planet Earth with her radiant green eyes, sweet freckles, and dense reddish-blond hair stayed at the back of his mind. He wished to meet Ina to get to know her. What would Rida, his wannabe girlfriend, say to that? She was firmly convinced that Farres and she were meant for each another. He never had the courage to tell her the truth about the complete lack of feelings he had for her. He had enjoyed a bit too much her acquaintance, the acceptance, and all the other advantages resulting from her wealthy parents.

'Stop dreaming!' Farres was startled and turned around. He hadn't seen his brother silently stalking him.
'Alons! What do you want?'
'You have told Xio a really idiotic story!'
'Don't complain! It was you who wreaked havoc', Farres countered furiously.
'I owed Sesa a favor.'
'Really?' Farres asked with surprise. 'Which one?'
'That's none of your business', his brother replied. 'It was you who broke our agreement. How could you tell Xio that Sesa fooled you! I know you, and I think you like

that terrestrial girl too much!'
Farres didn't respond.
'Maybe it's your bad conscience', Alons went on. 'You are to blame for Ina's awkward situation. That thing with the space ship…'
'Shut up!' Farres shouted at him.
'And what's going on with Rida? Two girlfriends can be a heavy burden', Alons said grinning.
'You're silly', Farres said annoyed.
'Would you like some good advice?' Alons asked after a minute.
'No!' replied Farres.
'Break up with Rida. She neither suits you nor our family. I think our parents are right.'
For a moment Farres looked at his brother.
'You aren't afraid of her, are you?' Alons knew that he was right. Voluntarily nobody liked to start an argument with Rida.

Ina swam for her life. Soon after she had dived down, her surroundings disappeared in total darkness. She didn't know these waters and could only orient herself with the help of the lightning bolts illuminating the water for a fraction of a second. If one of them struck the water surface near her, it could mean her death. No, she had to reach the bottom of the lake. Hopefully it was deep enough.

Ina didn't pay attention to the fact that she was breathing through her gills. It was more important to save her life. Perhaps she'd discover a niche in the rock bed or something else on the bottom of the lake, where she could take shelter. After some anxious minutes she could feel the sand under her searching hands. Very well, but what could she do now? Above the thunderstorm was raging, but down here it was quiet. She longed to pause for breath, but the troublesome buoyancy stopped her from doing so. She had to keep moving constantly to hold her position. Yeah, the crazy doctor had not considered that…

Far away a point of light was softly pulsating and dancing up and down attracting Ina's attention. Even from its great distance it radiated warmth and peace. It attracted Ina like a magnet, and she approached it. The light grew bigger, divided itself, and adopted form and color. Wonderful creatures emerged from the darkness. No, Ina wasn't afraid. She didn't mind being surrounded by a dozen of them.

'Hallo Ina! Welcome!'

An ice-cold shudder ran down her spine. This tender voice calling her name was in her head. Did she suffer from hallucinations? It definitely seemed as if she was losing her mind.
'We are real, Ina. Here on the bottom of the Loki Lake you are safe from the thunderstorm.' Finally Ina dared to look directly at the creatures. Their dark eyes softly looked at her; their snouts had big nostrils. Most striking were their pointy, movable ears and the long, orange color, wavy manes. Ina was reminded of horses, her favorite animals. Although this species was adapted to life under water, the form of their head and body resembled terrestrial creatures. The scaled skin of these water dwellers was shimmering in turquoise color. Slowly the creatures drew closer to her.
'We are Iaos', purred the voice in Ina's mind. 'We communicate telepathically; you can perceive our thoughts.' Meanwhile Ina was able to discern every detail. The Iaos were a little bigger than Ina and they seemed to shine from their interior filling the darkness of the water with diffuse light. It had a tranquilizing effect on her. Even when she touched an Iao's mane, she wasn't frightened; on the contrary, Ina enjoyed the touch and closed her eyes.
'You belong to your equals and you have to go back. We're going to bring you back to them.'
'Why did they want to bring her back?' Ina thought. She felt a slight panic. She was staring into the eyes of one of the Iaos. It was just an inch away from her face.
'Calm down, terrestrial girl. You are exhausted and longing for rest and sleep. Don't fight against it. Everything will be all right. Trust us!'

Ina dreamt of the lake and of the wonderful living creatures she had met. Strange enough, in her dream she tried to follow the Iaos while she was diving. However, she wasn't able to move forward. Her surroundings became gradually darker and more threatening. Bizarre faces appeared in front of her. Cold and fear alternated with warmth and peace. Flashes of lightning illuminated ghostly grimaces. Ina opened her eyes up wide. Where was she? She was staring at a blue ashlar as tall as a man just a few inches away from her. She wanted to touch it and move it away from her. But for some reason she wasn't able to move. Did the Iaos do this to her? No, they were peaceful, weren't they? But apparently they had brought her back. Ina listened carefully into the silence. Meanwhile that monotonous noise was familiar to her. She was in the laboratory again. Once more she tried to tense her muscles or at least to lift up the head, but she seemed to be paralyzed. An ice-cold fear took hold of her. What was happening with her?
'The Yso-Syrup is very effective' Ronok said all of a sudden. Ina was terrified and wished to turn her face to him, but she couldn't move at all. Not to be able to see her supposed enemy and just hearing his voice was terrible.
'You'll be unable to move for a couple of hours. This will be a sort of lesson for your incredible foolishness.'
What? Why? It was not her fault at all; she just had followed her sister!
'To participate in Sesa's silly plan was really naïve, but I didn't expect anything else of you. Even for a trained

sportsman it's much too far to swim from the palace to Rambala, especially during the worst thunderstorm.' Ronok paused for a moment, and then he added angrily: 'I wonder if you know that you almost destroyed a lifelong dream of mine and the entire work of the last years.'
Without previous warning Ronok sealed Ina's mouth and nose with a sort of mask. Ina gasped desperately. Was Ronok miserably choking her to death? She began to breathe painfully with the gills supplying her with oxygen.
'Do you know that you could have killed our daughter together with you? Do you have no compassion at all?' Ronok asked furiously.
The pungent pricking in her sides drove tears into her eyes and sweat out of her pores. Each breath produced a dreadful pain. In the lake it had been a completely different feeling.
'That hurts, right? You hopefully keep this in mind. If you have any chance to escape again, you should better think it over very well.'
Why did he torture her? Was it the punishment for her unsuccessful attempt to escape? Why for heaven's sake had the Iaos brought her back?
She didn't see Maris who came rushing to her bed. She contemplated the terrestrial girl in disbelief, stroking consolingly over her hair. When she noticed that Ina could not even move, she shouted at her husband: 'What did you do to her?'
Ronok didn't say a word. She cast a killing glance at him and took the mask off Ina's face carefully. 'It's all right, baby, I'll clarify this and you can rest now.' This time Ina took the soporific voluntarily. She wished to forget, just fall asleep and not wake up anymore…
'I just can't believe it! I hope you have a reasonable explanation for me!' Ronok turned away from his wife without a word.
'You've given her the Yso-Syrup, didn't you?' Maris said

desperately. But she was fervently hoping to be wrong.
'It was necessary, darling. She would have defended herself.'
'Why didn't you make your tests while she was sleeping, eh? You know exactly that it is very painful for Ina to breathe through the gills, when she's connected to the machine, don't you?' Maris asked furiously.
She took a cloth and dried the young woman's pale face.
'It was indispensable.'
'Yes, for sure. Do you want to know what I think?' Maris shouted at her husband. 'You just wanted to punish her for the attempt of escape.'
For a moment Ronok was quiet, and then he declared resigning: 'She just received a lesson. Beings like her need rigorous measures to comprehend.'
'You intentionally tortured her.' Maris slumped down into an armchair looking despicably at Ronok. 'Ina is a human being and…'
'Come on, stop it!' grumbled Ronok. 'She is a creature from a distant substandard planet. Apart from her anatomy, she has nothing to do with us.' Ronok hated arguing with his wife. Maris had a lot of compassion for Ina, and that was always leading to trouble.
'Don't you understand that you're committing a serious mistake? Ina will never trust us.' Maris swept over her forehead.
'If she doesn't, it won't matter anyway.'
'Did you actually think of our daughter only once?' she asked, her voice choked with tears.
'I constantly do.'
'Shora no longer has a survival chance. Ina won't want to help us anymore.'
'That's nonsense! Soon she'll be diving for the Gaia-fruits.'
'Are you going to force her?'
'I think she's understood today's message. If not, I'll have to think about other suitable means.'

'What have you become?' Maris shook her head and sighed. She couldn't go on like this. She had to take immediate action. She had no choice.
Maris stood up, pressed he hands into her hips, and said with an icy voice: 'From this moment on I want you to leave Ina alone!'
'What?' Ronok looked at her, as if she were mad. 'How will this be possible?'
'You're going to transfer Ina's medical care over to us: To Ana, Liess, and me!'
'Ana?'
'She has witnessed all the intervention and knows all about the experiment.'
'I don't think that's a good idea. Ana is still very young and…'
'Or you agree, or…' Maris thought for a moment. Her eyes wandered over to the window. The sky was deep blue now; there was no sign of yesterday's thunderstorm. 'Or we'll separate!'
'You can't do that!'
'I have to', Maris said with a sigh. She turned away and broke into tears.

The next days were a challenge for everybody who had to deal with Ina. She was no longer accessible, yelled if somebody approached her, ate almost nothing, and stared into the distance. She panicked at the smallest sound because she believed Ronok was entering the laboratory. Maris assured her several times that her husband had to stay away from her, but it was to no avail. In the beginning, to care for Ina, for example changing the Quados was only possible when she was fast asleep.

Ana, a young and ambitious Sathorjan woman, could finally convince Ina to accept her situation, and she recovered her will to live. The two young women were sitting together and talking for hours looking out of the panorama window. When Ina finally was willing to talk about her fears and sorrows, Ana listened to her. She for herself talked openly about her life on Sathorja and the advantages of living there.

'Oh, by the way', said Ana one day as if it wasn't important at all, 'Farres would like to see you again.'

Ina looked at her with surprise. For a moment, Ana's flashing blue eyes blinked, and a smile scurried in her well-proportioned face. She had tied together her long, wavy, light blonde hair. She looked roguish, and one could be certain she was 'a good sport'…

'Therefore you should learn at last to accept yourself as you are now. Otherwise they'll never let you out of the lab. I don't think it's very romantic, when Farres has to visit you in here. Such a first date needs another kind of ambience', said Ana smiling.

Thoughtfully Ina looked out of the window and didn't reply.
'This experiment complicates your life a little.'
Ina shook her head with annoyance.
'Listen! To change the Quados is simple, and there's not much more to observe. Anyway, your fluid intake is perfectly regulated by your body.' Ana paused for a moment; then she went on in a lower voice: 'Oh yes, you have to dive every three days for a couple of hours, in order to keep your gills functioning.'
'I beg your pardon?'
'You should get used to it as soon as possible. If you don't go into the water for one reason or the other, you'll find yourself back in the laboratory soon. You already know Ronok's machines and…'
'But don't be afraid, Ina. You definitely won't have to go through this procedure with full consciousness again', Ana quickly added.
Less than a day later the experiment didn't seem to disturb Ina anymore. Gill breathing was explained to her as well as the use of the Quados, and she didn't mind. The instruction about the use of the countless functions of the CC3 was more difficult. Ina asked so many questions that Ana had to call her friend Okon for help. On the end, Ina understood more or less the microcomputer's tasks. She especially appreciated its memory functions. From now on they would serve her well. Familiar with her weaknesses, she knew exactly that in the beginning she tended to forget the new but important essentials of life.
In the late afternoon, shortly before Ina's discharge from the laboratory she seemed silent and preoccupied. Liess had come to talk to her. She had brought her an exquisite flower dish, but Ina neither wanted to eat nor listen to Liess' stories.
'What's wrong with you, my baby?' the old lady asked like a grandmother. 'Are you worried? Tomorrow you'll

start a new and independent life. That's a reason to be happy and face the future optimistically.' Ina shook her head morosely.
'What's depressing you?' Liess wanted to know.
Ina turned to the old lady.
'Why did they choose me to save that woman Shora? I'm only a human being. I'm not able do such a thing. I'm not a good swimmer and I hate diving.'
'You can swim; you already proved it. All the rest you will learn.'
'But why exactly did they choose me?' Ina asked again.
'It was a series of unfortunate events, my dear. Consider it to be a coincidence and a chance.'
'I beg your pardon?'
'You know that Sesa made them bring you here, don't you?'
Ina nodded.
'Well, unfortunately many things went wrong. One of the pilots of the space shuttle switched off the invisibility mode for a moment and caused your terrible bicycle accident.'
'Did I have an accident?' Ina asked confused.
'You fell so badly that you wouldn't have survived on Earth. Xio asked Ronok to take care of you. You have to know that he's a brilliant physician. Well, Ronok saw his chance to save Shora. So he asked Xio on his part to allow him to use you for his experiment. Unfortunately due to your origin you are without any rights here; so Xio agreed and handed you over to the doctor as his property.' Liess took a breather. Then she slowly went on:
'You must know that Ronok was looking for volunteers for his experiment for weeks, but nobody wanted to run the risk.'
'Sure!' Ina sighed. 'But why does he need people? There must be super-modern devices on Sathorja working more precisely than people.'

'Oh, certainly there are. Unfortunately three diving robots broke down when they were trying to get Gaia-fruits.'
'What? And now I shall do that?' Ina shouted aghast.
'Yes, that's right. Ronok ran out of money, and he couldn't buy any more robots.'
'And this experiment didn't cost anything?' Ina wondered.
'It did, my dear. It was extremely expensive, but Ronok has been able to find sponsors who supported him. I suppose they thought it would be interesting to implant gills into a human being.'
'It would have been cleverer to find people to finance another diving robot.'
'Well, I don't want to talk about this', said the Sathorjan woman and stood up clumsily. 'I'll have to leave you now. I wish you a wonderful start into your new life.' With a twinkle in her eye she scuffled out of the laboratory.
Ina sat alone, thoughtfully looking out of the window on the colorful trees. On a branch a little animal clambered about. It looked like a squirrel; however, it had no fur, but a pink skin. Suddenly it got frightened, fell down many yards into a bush, and disappeared.
'These Nunos are swift animals.'
Ina turned around startled. Without previous warning, Farres was suddenly standing behind her.
'It's you!' she stammered perplexed. Ana had told her the truth. She didn't dare to look at the young man. His presence caused her heart to beat wildly. What was the purpose of his surprise visit? Had he been ordered to come, so she would get used and adapt to the new situation?'
'Sorry, if I frightened you', Farres said quickly. He sounded a little embarrassed. When he sat down close to her, her cheeks turned uncomfortably red.
'How do you like it here?' began Farres after a prolonged silence. What an embarrassing question!

'Don't know', replied Ina in a low voice briefly looking up. Their eyes met for a fraction of a second.
'In fact I wanted to apologize to you.'
'Do you?' she asked puzzled.
'I alerted the security department.' Farres didn't look at her. 'The thunderstorm looked dangerous and…' He stopped abashed.
'The Iaos brought me back to shore, so what you did, doesn't matter for me', replied Ina. She wasn't really convinced of what she was saying.
'Did they? Presumably these creatures thought you belonged to us, and that you'd feel comfortable here with us', reasoned Farres.
'Do you think so?' Ina asked amazed.
'If the Iaos had suspected that you'd suffer, they wouldn't have brought you back. People say they're never wrong.'
'I'm not so sure', Ina said with a deep sigh.
Farres looked at Ina with a guilty conscience. Hadn't he talked nonsense just now?
Ina fought against the tears. She didn't want to start weeping in the presence of the young man. She had to be strong without showing any weakness. But she couldn't prevent the tears from running down her reddened cheeks. She swept them away with a quick movement of her hand.
'I heard that Ronok has given you Yso-Syrup. He should not have done that', said Farres compassionately and took her in his arms. Normally Ina wouldn't let a complete stranger to hug her, but in her pain she allowed it. She shut her eyes and enjoyed the momentary protection.
Neither Farres nor Ina had noticed Maris, Ronok, and Ana who were standing behind a big machine observing the scene.
'Come on, we have to let the two alone', Maris said urging Ronok and trying to pull him away. He shook his head. 'No, we have to separate them immediately.'
'But why should we?' Maris asked annoyed.

'Because they're a bad match', he shouted displeased. Ina ceased embracing Farres as she saw Ronok rapidly approaching her. Where could she go?
'Don't be afraid!' Farres whispered in her ear. 'He won't get close to you; I'll see to it.' He stood up, putting himself in front of the terrestrial girl.
'What's the point of that?' Ronok asked angrily. 'Why are you here?'
'Because I wished to see Ina', the Sathorjan replied.
'You already did so, you can go now.'
'I won't go anywhere', said Farres stubbornly.
'Please darling, leave Ina and Farres alone!' Maris followed her husband, as did Ana who was anxiously watching the situation. 'Remember our agreement. You promised me to keep away from Ina, when she's conscious.'
Ronok took a deep breath, thought for a while, and then he said: 'This here is an exception. Such a rhapsody keeps Ina away from her actual task and confuses her. She'll put my experiment in danger and I can't allow that. Moreover, it's as clear as daylight that this will never work with these two anyway. Xio won't tolerate this dalliance, neither will I nor Rida.'
Farres cast a furious look at Ronok. He turned to Ina who was sitting on the bed. She was trembling, looking helplessly and miserable. Her green eyes stared at the doctor; she was prepared to run away, if he had come any nearer. Her face had turned snow white, and her long reddish-blonde hair fell stringily over her sloping shoulders.
'Since Ina is legally an object and part of my property, I dispose hereby and from now on that these two must not meet again', said Ronok. 'I'll clarify all the necessary measures with Xio and Losos.'
As he said this, Maris got into a rage and shouted: 'You don't seriously think you have the right to interfere in these people's privacy?'
'That's exactly what I'm doing.'

Maris shook her head desperately. How could he have changed so much? Where was the man she had married? Next to her stood a selfish, ignorant, intolerant, and cruel man she really didn't want to be involved with.
'Damn Ronok, you can't do that! You are totally crazy!' shouted Farres furiously.
'Who's getting crazy here? You should care about Rida before you try to start a new relationship!' Ronok cried out indignantly.
With every word Ina's confusion increased even more.
'Why do you constantly mention her? I'll break up with her. From now on I want to meet with Ina to get to know her. These things happen. It also happened with Maris and you, even though it's very long time ago, and you already forgot about it.'
'You shouldn't have said that!' Maris sighed sadly. Oh yes, Ronok and her had fallen in love head over heels. At that time Maris had left her boyfriend Garos because of Ronok. That was thirty five years ago, but now?
'That doesn't matter. I don't need your or somebody else's permission. I'll continue meeting Ina, and you won't be able to impede it.' Farres turned away, sat down on the bed next to Ina, and put his arm on her shoulder. Ina got frightened at his touch, but a second later she gratefully clung to him.
'You can think whatever you want', Ronok said coldly.
'Don't you understand? Ina needs Farres.' remarked Ana. So far she had listened in silence, but now she had to intervene. 'She needs somebody she can trust.'
'That's nonsense!'
'Ina obviously feels fine with him', Ana went on unswervingly. 'She can sit quietly on the bed, although you are close to her. This is quite amazing after all you did to her.'
'Ana, if you want to go on working in my team, you better shut up', the doctor spat at her. Then he watched carefully the young couple. It was true: Ina felt secure with

Farres. She was calming down more and more. That was strange. Maybe Ana was right, and Ina really needed somebody like Farres at her side. She would settle down faster, could harvest the fruit earlier, and so be able to save Shora.

'Please, darling!' said Maris with a begging look. 'Give them a chance! What difference does it make?'

'What a question!' Ronok shouted. 'Ina is from Earth and Farres is Sathorjan. They are worlds apart.'

'And light years', remarked Ana.

'It doesn't matter', Ronok said sighing after a long break. 'In my opinion, all this is a mistake.' He paused again and then he said resigning: 'They shall try with each other.'

Everybody looked at him.

'I beg your pardon?' Maris asked completely caught by surprise. No, she hadn't expected that.

'But I impose conditions', added the doctor. 'Farres, you'll immediately inform Rida and Xio about your wish to be together with Ina. Hopefully Rida will understand your sudden affection and doesn't see her as a rival. Furthermore, I expect you to ensure that Ina deals reasonably with my experiment without doing foolish things.' Ronok thought for a moment, and then he said: 'In about two weeks, Ina shall dive for fruits in the Loki Lake. The acclimatization period will be over then. You will still be told the exact day. The day before, she has to come to the laboratory for a discussion and some final tests.'

'What? I have to bring Ina here, so you can torture her again?' Farres asked enraged.

'She won't notice the tests, because she'll be sleeping. If everything is clear, I'll go back to my actual task now', he said, turned to one of his devices, and checked their indicators.

'Darling', stuttered Maris', 'I don't know what to say.'

'I did it exclusively for our daughter.'

Ina was not able to evaluate her feelings. Did she really have feelings for this unknown young man? Or did she just long for protection and security, no matter who they came from?
Lost in thoughts she stuffed a light blue flower into her mouth observing Farres who was talking to Ana and Maris in a low voice. Hadn't she lately told Eva she was fed up with men? 'Oh, Eva', she said to herself and sighed, 'what had happened to her? Was she still living alone or had she finally found somebody?'
'Ina?' Maris sat down next to her and said cautiously: 'My husband would like to talk to you.'
Ina turned around looking for Farres. He was still talking to Ana a couple of yards away.
'It won't take long', Maris added quickly. 'And he'll stay where he is, all right?' Indeed Ronok kept at a distance and talked to her calmly and patiently for the first time: 'You can leave the laboratory any time you wish. Finally you are ready to try your luck outside of these four walls. If you have any problems, speak to Maris or Ana.'
Ina nodded hesitantly.
'Ina, if I find out that you are consciously ruining my experiment by putting your and our daughter's life in danger, you can expect serious consequences. Do you understand?'
'Yes', Ina whispered almost inaudibly. She couldn't avoid a slight trembling.
'Have you just threatened her?' Farres asked enraged.
'Yes', replied Ronok coldly and left the lab.
'Ina saw him leaving the room and she didn't dare to breathe again, until he had gone.
'Don't worry, Ina', said Maris with a sigh, 'I'll make sure that he leaves you alone.'
'You have survived the worst', Ana said with a wry smile. 'Slowly it's getting better. Well, I'm going home now.'
'All right Ana, thank you', said Maris and stood up.

'Do you want me to show you your apartment, Ina?' Farres asked a little later, took her hand, and pulled her on her feet.
'Yes please!' she said beaming with joy. She was happy, and the black clouds Ronok's threat had left in her soul disappeared at once being replaced by sunshine and amorousness.
'Sesa will pick you up shortly', Maris said and looked at her CC3.
'Oh no!' Ina thought disenchanted. She had forgotten completely.
'Then you have to wait for her', Farres said, kissed her on her cheek and left the laboratory.

'What's wrong with you?' Sesa asked confused, when she saw Ina waiting all alone. 'You look so unwelcoming.'
'Do you think?' replied Ina, stood up and followed Sesa into the corridor flooded with light. A transport robot was waiting for them: Ina climbed on the platform with a gentle swing, sat down behind Sesa, and held fast.
Before we go, I want to know what happened', Sesa asked curiously.
'You didn't visit me a single time!' Ina burst out. 'Do you know how bad it was being defenseless at the mercy of Ronok? He punished me, Sesa. I think I did nothing wrong. I just listened to you!'
Sesa had turned to her sister. She was desperate and didn't say a word.
'If Maris hadn't come to help me, I would have died from the pain. You can't imagine', Ina sobbed. 'Yes, before Ronok has been in the lab, and without Farres…'
'Farres has been with you?' Sesa asked astonished.
'Yes.' Ina noticed her face getting uncomfortably hot.
'Oh no, Ina, you like him, don't you?'
Ina didn't answer. Sesa started the transporter; the vehicle lifted off the floor and floated along the wide corridor. This time Sesa was driving more slowly and carefully. She seemed to be lost in her thoughts. Ina thought Sesa's reaction was a little weird. Normally she would have asked a lot of questions and enjoyed the sightseeing tour through the palace. But today she didn't.
'We have arrived', said Sesa in an unaccented voice and climbed down from the transporter. Ina followed her.

She noticed that they were in a huge dome hall.
Ina turned around her own axis and was fascinated. She had never seen such a fantastic thing: A crystal hall reflecting the disappearing sunlight. There were arm chairs, tables, flowering plants, and strange furniture apparently without any function floating around the hall.
'That's magnificent', she murmured, 'but where are we? Where is my flat?' She looked around searching. No exit, no doors, nothing was indicating another room.
'My parents will be here soon', said Sesa.
'What? Why? I thought you would bring me to my new home', Ina said panting disillusioned.
'They want to talk to you, and I think I know now why.'
'Here?' Ina asked and looked around again. For a private conversation the hall looked quite inconvenient. Human beings and aliens were arriving little by little making Ina feel confined.
'Not here, Ina. We are waiting to enter the private section.' Sesa pointed to a mirrored wall which Ina hadn't noticed before. 'My father is an important personality, and therefore we have to comply with a specific protocol.'
Ina went away from her sister wandering leisurely between the chairs and looking out of the panorama window. Many yards below them, extensive meadows and forests lay in the light of the setting suns. Far away an emerald blue band was sparkling, a river, perhaps an inflow to the lake? Shadowy mountains were visible in the haze, if you looked at them long enough. What an enchanted, colorful world. For a single fleeting moment Ina thought she was dreaming. It was simply impossible that so many crazy things, which had happened to her, were real.
'Ina, I'm very sorry', Sesa voice sounded right behind her. 'I didn't want all this to happen. I'm racked by remorse because of my stupid idea and I thought you probably didn't want to see me.'

She wasn't completely wrong…
Sesa hugged her sister and whispered: 'Please, forgive me.'
'It's all right. Anyway I have met Farres.'
'For heaven's sake, you better stay away from him,' Sesa said panting.
'Why?'
'He may be quite nice, but his girlfriend is completely insane.'
'Rida?'
'Yes, that's her name. How do you know about her?'
'Ronok told me.'
'What?'
'He used her as a way to pressure me. In the beginning he was against…' Ina suddenly stopped.
'What are you talking about?'
'Farres has fallen in love with Ina.' Startled the young women looked back. Xio, Sesa's adoptive father, stood behind them and was listening to their conversation. He was a medium sized, stubby man with a rigid face who seldom smiled; he always seemed to be sorrowful. His mind was under increasing pressure due to his political position. He loved his daughter and was concerned about her, but also often unnerved.
'Why does everybody know, only I don't?' Sesa complained in a loud voice.
'A moment ago, Farres has come to see me. He informed me that he wished to become more familiar with your sister', her father replied.
'What? That just can't be true', Sesa said gasping. 'These two only met once!'
'They already met twice, my darling!' Bora remarked.
'Hallo Mum!' Sesa hugged her adoptive mother.
'It's nice that you come to visit us, Ina', she said to the terrestrial girl. 'Please, come with us.'
Bora led the sisters to a mirrored wall. Ina stopped irritated. She couldn't see any door opening. Bora passed

through the mirror like a ghost and disappeared.
'But…' Ina stared at the mirror wall unable to say a word.
'That's just an optical illusion, Ina. Don't worry. Come with us!' Xio said. Then he also disappeared into the wall.
'Sesa!' Ina was panicking, but her sister had just gone through the mirror, too. Helplessly Ina looked around in the hall. Nobody had noticed her apart from a group of yellow aliens with green eyes. 'Oh my God', murmured Ina.
When one of these creatures stood up and began to waddle toward her, Ina mustered all her courage, closed her eyes, and quickly passed through the mirror. There was no impact, no splintering glass, just nothing. Ina was in an entrance hall full of plants. She had to be careful not to step on the flowers. The splendor spread an inebriant fragrance. Ina pushed aside a big leaf which was blocking her view. Where had her hosts gone?
'Ina, there you are at last', Sesa called her from the bottom of the stairs. 'Come on, we have to go up several floors.'
Ina followed Sesa, puffing. With each step she noticed that her body was in bad shape. She wasn't fit at all. Maybe it was because of the experiment. Didn't Ronok tell her, her lungs had less capacity now in favor of the gills?
'Smoker's lungs; how nice', Ina thought unhappily.
'Ina, are you all right?'
'How can your parents do this every day?' Ina asked gasping. 'How could they hurry ahead so fast?'
'They went up with a transporter', replied Sesa.
'And we have to walk?' Ina gasped. 'I always do.' Sesa said. 'I hate the vertical ascent with the robot.'
Ina went on trotting slowly and took a couple of breaks in between. Ten minutes later they finally reached Xio and Boras apartment.
'It took you very long', Bora said, when she saw the sisters. 'Just pass over to the dining room. Dinner has already been served.'
'Okay, Mom.'

Ina could hardly believe what she saw: The flat was like a palace from a fairy tale. Again the principal elements were glass and light. The Sathorjans seemed to love this. When Ina entered the generous dining room, she remained rooted to the spot. A pond surrounded by plants attracted her attention. She could hear the gentle splash of streaming water and a marvelous chant. But where did it come from? Ina looked around searching, and she discovered many tiny little creatures in the water and on the flowers. They were shimmering in the sunlight in all rainbow colors. Their smooth skin was squamous and they had six legs holding to the culms in the air and in the water.

'What kind of animals are these?' Ina asked fascinated. She wasn't afraid at all. These creatures with their wonderful chant seemed to be peaceful and soothing.

'These are little Gunars. They aren't indigenous here, they only live with the human beings who care for them', explained Bora patiently.

'They are wonderful', Ina said enchanted.

'I know.'

'Mom wanted a little bit of nature by all means', Sesa said shrugging. She didn't fancy green oases in the living room.

'I love to sit here when the weather is bad, Ina.' Bora pointed to a very comfortable seat group. 'But now it's time for supper.'

The table was floating in a convexity, and it was overloaded with delicious flower dishes. Ina was already used to the Sathorjan kitchen which was exclusively vegetarian. She had completely forgotten the taste of meat and didn't think of the Earth very often anymore.

Ina sat down on a soft, comfortable chair and felt extremely tired. It had been a hard day.

'Please, serve yourself, Ina!' Bora said motherly.

'Thank you', murmured the young woman and let her gaze wander over the delicacies.

'You'll settle down here quickly.' Bora sat down opposite the girls next to her husband and poured juice into each of the tall, narrow glasses. Without previous warning a hairy fluffy ball raced over the table, knocking down Ina's glass, and landing gently in Bora's exuberant head of hair. Ina looked startled at the Sathorjan. What a funny creature was this? At this very moment Bora looked as if she had two heads and four eyes. 'My goodness, Kuni, what are you doing?' She carefully took the fluffy ball from her head, caressed it softly and put it on the table.
Ina couldn't bring out a single word while she cast a frightened look at the creature. It was looking at Ina with his google eyes producing a soft curr.
'That's a Knudi, Ina', explained Sesa. 'He's one of my parents' pets. He's harmless, cuddly, easy to care for, and incredibly sweet.'
Ina did not think the basketball size animal was cute. His dense, hairy, and violet fur and his mouth with pointy teeth frightened her. No, she didn't want to caress that creature. She didn't understand how he could float. He had no wings and his six extremities were rather tiny.
'I think he likes you!' Sesa took Kuni carefully in both hands and passed him over to Ina.
'Caress him', she prompted her sister. Horrified Ina stared at the purring thing. He had focused his eyes on her with an imploring look.
'Please, he likes it.'
Bora approached Ina, took her hand, and guided her over the Knudi's fur. The animal enjoyed it and closed his eyes.
'You can talk to him. He understands everything and knows your feelings', Bora explained. 'He's really a treasure.' Kuni confirmed this with a chuckling noise. Ina ran her fingers through his fluffy hair again. It had a silky, soft, and warm touch and a calming effect.
'You're a little sweetheart', she murmured.
The Knudi stood up and floated along her arm until he

landed on her shoulder.
'He really likes you.' Sesa was happy.
'That's very nice, but unfortunately I have to send him away, so we can have supper in peace.' Bora had correctly interpreted her husband's look, picked up Kuni, and whispering some soft words to him. The Knudi disappeared instantaneously as quickly as he had turned up.
Sesa and her mother were still talking about the advantages of the Knudis, when Ina noticed Xio's thoughtfulness.
Xio had to face a conflict. The fact that Farres had officially admitted his inclination to Ina caused him a strong headache. A Sathorjan who was together with a girl without rights from Earth could cause a lot of problems. Some of the delegates of the community would not agree with it. Some of them would reason and demand to change the law at last accepting relationships between creatures of different origin. In addition to that, Rida's family had great influence and maintained good relations to one of the chairmen. Xio was certain that Rida and her parents soon would complain... Anyway, it was quite strange that Ronok was now on Ina and Farres' side as were most of residents of the palace. The news had spread quickly.
'What shall I do?' Xio murmured to himself. Ina cast a frightened look at him, but then she went on devoting herself to the delicious flower dish.
Xio was contemplating Ina thoughtfully. Essentially she was a poor, unfortunate girl. Her only flaw was her terrestrial origin. He had no right to destroy their tender love. Farres' intentions were sincere; he even would risk his job in the security department for her. Well, maybe he could adopt Ina, if Ronok was willing to let her go. Then he would have two terrestrial adoptive daughters. He knew for sure that Bora would be happy. But would the delegates of the Council agree with the adoption?
'Darling, you seem so absentminded', Bora said to her husband. She was worried.

'Well, you know why', replied Xio shaking his head. Bora looked briefly at Ina. Just a minute later she asked him tentatively: 'Darling, have you taken a decision yet?'
Xio looked seriously from one to the other, nodded, and said: 'Ina, you may go on meeting with Farres. That's all right for me.'
'That's great!' Sesa said happily. But then she paused and looked concerned: 'But Dad, what about Rida? She will be lovesick and lay the blame on Ina. She is still firmly convinced that Farres loves her.'
'Leave that to me. I'll take care of it.'
Bora hugged her husband and kissed him. 'That's the right decision, darling. I'm proud of you. You follow your heart and act on behalf of Ina.'
'Thank you', murmured Ina. She was abashed, her cheeks were deep red, and her eyes were sparkling. She couldn't believe that Xio just like Ronok was going to allow the budding relationship between Farres and her. Those two old gentlemen were giving them a real chance!
'Pardon me, but I'd like to ask a question', Ina began to say uncertainly. 'Who is Rida?'
'She's Bro and Tenia's daughter, wealthy businessmen. They have several boutiques in our largest shopping promenade', Bora explained patiently. 'They have invested a lot of money in the expansion of this building and have co-determination rights in economic decisions concerning Sathorja. In short, they are influential, and Farres has used her to move up into higher circles. He visited many parties with her, made lots of contacts, and enjoyed his life. With all those excesses he didn't take in account that Rida considered him her boyfriend.'
'He doesn't like Rida!' Sesa said quickly when she saw her sister's gaze.
'Everything changed abruptly when he saw you for the first time in the space ship', said Bora.
'I don't understand that', Ina said looking from one to the other.

'She doesn't know, Mom', Sesa hissed.
'What?' Ina asked confused.
'It's nothing.' Sesa tried to downplay the situation.
'Ina', Xio began to explain. 'Farres was one of the pilots of that space shuttle that took you to Sathorja.
'Ah yes?' Ina swallowed. She remembered Liess' words and began to suspect what would come now. 'Does that mean that Farres made a mistake?'
'It was an accident', Bora quickly said. 'Do not take this the wrong way, Ina. Surely his feelings have nothing to do with compassion or a bad conscience.'
Ina cast a doubtful look at her. Why had everything to be so complicated?
After a moment of silence, Ina said to Sesa in a low voice: 'Could you please show me the apartment now! I am terribly tired; today was a very tough day.'
'With pleasure', Sesa said and stood up. 'Mom, Dad, I'll take Ina to her flat now.'
'It's all right, Sesa.' Bora also rose, hugged her daughter and Ina, too. 'Everything will be all right, my baby', she whispered comfortingly.
Ina nodded, murmured a thank you for the invitation, said a well-behaved good bye to Xio, and followed her sister.

Ina woke up after a restless night in an unfamiliar room. She quickly sat up and looked around. It was a large, circular shaped room with huge panorama windows. Even the ceiling was partly transparent. The twin suns had already reached the zenith. Ina looked at her CC3. It was short before noon. She climbed out of her bed. Yes, she could remember that she had gone to bed in the bedroom of her own home. Alone at last! Happily she went around in circles. Suddenly a loud and dazzling beep filled the room and made her shudder. She needed a couple of seconds, until she understood that it came from her CC3. She had to change urgently her Quados and drink water. The young woman looked around. Where for heaven's sake might be the bathroom? How would she find her way in this flat? There was a staircase opposite her bed leading to the ground floor. No, only the living room and the entrance hall were downstairs. She tried to remember Sesa's words. The bathroom had to be upstairs. Big plants with flowers covered most of the wall. Ina proceeded systematically pronouncing commands and walking around in circles. She discovered another room full up with clothes, shoes and fashionable accessories. The alarm sounded again. She had to ask somebody. Sesa?
Ok. But how could she contact her with that stupid microcomputer? Simply speak loudly or think?
Ina tried to do both things, but in vain. Only now she noticed an oval door opening on the right side next to the big window. When she entered it, she found herself in a huge bathroom. It was covered with mirrored surfaces,

an impressing basin, several wardrobes containing funny things, a toilet, and – but damn, where was the container for the Quados? Ina was getting nervous. If Ronok learned about it, she would certainly be punished again. A cold shiver ran down her spine when she remembered that her CC3 was connected with the computer in the laboratory constantly providing medical data…

It was peeping once again, louder and more penetrating than before. She had to take action. Ina cast a short look on the oversized bathtub, took off her night gown and the Quados, and climbed into the pool. She quickly immersed and noticed with relief that her special feature worked flawlessly. She relaxed while she swam through the basin measuring about ten by fifteen feet. She noticed that being in the water produced her great pleasure. She really was an amphibian now…

'Ina!' Ina could clearly hear somebody call her name and she also knew immediately whose voice it was.

After the alarm had sounded three times, Maris had managed to calm down Ronok and had rushed to the terrestrial girl's flat. Now she was standing in front of the basin in the bathroom and asked with concern: 'Everything all right?'

Ina clung to the basin rim and looked up to the Sathorjan with amazement.

'Darling', Maris shook her head. 'What did you do? Ronok is exasperated. With pain and misery I could convince him not to bring you back to the laboratory.'

'I couldn't find the bathroom and the container for the Quados', Ina explained sheepishly.

'Sesa didn't show it to you?' Maris asked surprised.

'Last night we have been very tired', replied Ina. 'I slept for a very long time and had little time to find my way around yet.'

'Yes, I know', Maris said and looked around. 'But where are your Quados now?' Just thinking of it and a container opened up in a niche. 'Well, you can come out now.

Farres is waiting in the living room and I think he's already been waiting quite a while. 'Farres?' A smile was beaming across Ina's face. Quickly she got out of the pool.
'Do you need any help?'
'No Maris, thank you.'
Ina needed more than an hour, until she came down the stairs to the living room. Drying and combing her dense, long hair with the automatic hairbrush was a challenge. The same happened, when she had to pick a fancy outfit. There was such a vast variety of clothes; she wasn't able to settle for one; she couldn't even get it off the coat hanger. Afterwards she had to look into the mirror for five minutes before she was ready to see Farres.
'Hallo Ina', the young man said joyfully. He approached her, stopped for a moment, and then embraced her. 'It's nice that you got ready at last', he added grinning. 'I beg your pardon', Ina stuttered and her cheeks reddened. 'Maris told me that you were waiting.
'That's okay', he said to sooth her, 'and only exceptionally I have time.'
'Tell me', Ina asked thoughtfully, 'can everybody come into my apartment, whenever he wants to?'
'No, usually you should lock the door.' Farres winked at her.
'Oh, I didn't think of it' Ina murmured embarrassedly.
Her eyes wandered from one window to the next and through the sun-drenched room.
'It's incredibly beautiful.' Large glass frontages, narrow walls, colorful plants, and a tasteful, comfortable sitting area adorned the huge room. Ina couldn't believe it. Her flat on Earth had been quite shabby. In a recess, there was even a table and four chairs standing firmly on the ground. 'Here I'm at home now'; she stammered. 'I can't believe it.'
A moment later, she thought about something else. She turned serious and thoughtful.
'Farres, may I ask you a question?'

'Yes, of course.'
'Do you really like me?'
'What are you talking about? What do you think? Why else should I be with you?'
'Yesterday Bora told me the story of the space ship', said Ina.
Farres didn't look at her. He let himself fall on the sofa and sighed.
Silently and insecurely, Ina sat down face to face with him.
'Yes, that's true', Farres said bitterly. 'It was an accident. That mistake has changed your whole life. I'm very sorry.'
Farres took a deep breath and tried to choose the right words.
'I would do anything I could to undo what happened.'
An uncomfortable silence arose. The room didn't appear so friendly anymore. It had grown a little darker; at least, that was how it seemed to Ina. Or was it a cloud covering the suns?
But all of a sudden, when the light flooded into the room again, Farres said: 'If you have the impression that I'm just interested in you because of my bad conscience, you are completely wrong!'
Ina didn't say anything. She really liked Farres so she just didn't want to think about it.
'I like you, Ina.'
'But we almost don't know each other!' replied Ina.
'It's just like this. You don't have to question everything! Do you know what I think? You have the same feeling for me. Even Ronok and Xio have noticed it.'
Ina didn't look at him. She stood up and went to the window. Farres followed her and put his hand on her shoulders.
'You must admit that you need me', he whispered into her ear.
Ina turned around and looked at him.

'I think so', she murmured.
When Farres kissed her tenderly, she closed her eyes and enjoyed it.
'I hope one day you'll be able to forgive me' he said.
'Do you mean the kiss?' Ina said and smirked.
'You know what I mean', Farres replied shaking his head. 'Come on, let's go out together. I have taken the day off today and I thought I might show you the palace.'
'With pleasure', Ina replied happily.
They went hand in hand along the corridor. It was the first time she noticed the vibrant life in the palace. They saw many people and other creatures on their long walk.
'We are leaving the residential area now', Farres explained. 'We're now approaching the entrance hall. – Be careful!' Coming out of nowhere, a transporter raced toward them. Ina pressed herself against the warm window screen waiting for it to pass.
'Hey, you can't fly around here like hell. This is a pedestrian zone', somebody scolded.
'I beg your pardon', Farres said to Ina. 'Some are really in a hurry, and they don't show consideration.'
'I know that', replied Ina. Suddenly she felt terribly hungry. 'Hmm, couldn't we get something to eat somewhere?'
'This is an excellent idea. In one of the shopping promenades there's one of the best restaurants we have. You'll like it.'
For half an hour, Ina went with Farres everywhere; walking downstairs along apparently endless corridors which partly offered spectacular views onto the outside world. And Ina never stopped; she walked on and on with just one goal: To satisfy her hunger.
'Where are we?' Ina moaned when they were crossing another huge hall.
'Look!' Farres pointed with his hand to a huge gate towering above all at a distance. 'That's where we met for the first time.'

'Oh, so we are at the entrance hall?'
'Actually we are in one of the extensions. The hall you mean starts at the glass wall surrounded by plants.'
Oh', said Ina when she became conscious of the real dimensions, 'why is everything so huge and made from glass?'
'Ina, you don't know the buildings in the Sathorjan cities yet. What you see here is rather small and claustrophobic.' Ina shook her head.
'Well, what you call glass is a highly developed building material. It's not just beautiful, but also very functional.'
Ina looked inquiringly at him.
'Well, that material is called Ips. It's transparent, but absolutely impermeable for cold and heat, almost indestructible, elastic, and unlimitedly formable. Very small things can be made of it, but also huge construction elements, just as you wish.'
'Wow!' Ina didn't know what to say.
'I don't know if you remember: The palace suddenly disappeared, when you walked down to the lake.'
Ina looked at Farres with surprise and nodded.
'That's one of the peculiarities of Ips. It merges with the surrounding landscape.'
'Is it found in nature?' Ina curiously asked.
'Oh no, it isn't. It's produced in factories. Some of the components come from natural raw materials, but they are melted down and refined. I don't know much more about it.'
'Interesting', said Ina and tried to ignore the rumble in her tummy.
Human beings and aliens, robots and transporters of all kind crossed their way. It was a big mess. Ina clenched Farres' hand, when they passed through a group of grey, red-eyed robots. One of them turned to her and said in a deep, rasping voice: 'Ina, you should get something to eat!'

Ina stopped abruptly and stared anxiously at the metallic creature.
'Ina, don't be afraid. There are even more robots here than humans and aliens together.'
'But this one knew my name!' Ina stammered.
'Well, it has logged itself into your CC3 and probably noticed that you have a very low blood glucose level.'
'Pardon me?'
'Just forget it. Don't think about it', Farres said with a wry smile.
Thoughtfully and silently, Ina walked beside Farres. Finally they reached a nice restaurant somehow separated from the hustle and protected by highly grown, flowering plants. They sat down at one of the little tables. Ina enjoyed the peace and looked around. Nobody had come to their table yet, but she suddenly discovered a dish of flower pie on the table. How she loved these delicious varieties! With a gentle hum, a floating ball robot put a narrow jar with water, a container, two plates, and one more dish on the table. Ina looked at the copper colored, shiny ball with dismay. Its tentacles looked like spider legs, membered and creepy. Ina moved her chair a little to the side to avoid it.
'Ina, what's wrong?' Farres asked startled. 'You look at it as if it were poisonous. It's just a primitive auxiliary robot.'
'I hate spiders', Ina gasped.
'What are you talking about?'
Ina noticed that her face was reddening. She sat straight upright and said: 'It doesn't matter.'
'You don't have to be afraid of those machines', Farres said shaking his head, took a little spoon-like shovel, and put some of the sweetishly fragrant flower pie on his plate.
'You know, on Earth…' Ina began.
'…everything is different', Farres completed her sentence and grinned.

Ina looked at him fretfully; then she also put some of the dish on her plate and began to eat.
'Wonderful', she said. 'It doesn't only look delicious; it also tastes good.'
'Yeah, our beloved Liess spoils us every day with her creations.'
'What? Does she prepare all these dishes? I can't believe it!'
'It's not her, but her robots. Come on, I'll show you the kitchen; it's really fascinating. Hmm, once you are here, you can also visit Liess. She has a lot to discuss with you anyway.'
Ina nodded unwillingly. She didn't want to think of her future task today. This would spoil her day.
'Oh yes, and then you should also pay a visit to Shora, Ronok's daughter. She's seriously ill therefore she's living next to Liess and…'
'What? She's here?'
'Sure, what did you think?
'I didn't know.' She really would have liked to change the topic. Slowly she went on eating.
'There you are! I tried to reach you all morning!' shouted a piercing female voice. A young woman made her way through the plants and cast an offended glance at Farres.
'What do you want, Rida?' Farres asked angrily. 'Don't you see that I'm busy?'
'Busy with this fish-woman?' Rida asked disdainfully. She was a little over twenty earth year old, had blonde, wavy hair reaching down to her waist, water-blue eyes, and a sensuous mouth. She easily might have been a model; she had the right size, measures and character, too – Ina supposed.
'Are you crazy? This is Ina, and you have to treat her with respect.'
'What? That slut from Earth? I don't really know why you like her.' She was eyeing Ina with disdain. 'She has red hair and green eyes. Who likes that? Oh, and she has

freckles in her cadaverous face!'
'Shut up!' Farres shouted furiously and threw an evil eye at Rida. 'You're lucky that I'm good at controlling mys-elf.'
'Are you? Do you want to attack me?' Rida asked offen-ded. 'How did she bewitch you? It's obvious that she cast her spell on you!'
'Nonsense, there is no spell at all.' He turned to Ina again. 'Don't listen to her. She's crazy', he remarked.
Now Ina began to understand, what Sesa had meant, when she mentioned Rida. This Sathorjan woman was nuts. She shook her head and turned to her meal again. She began to tell Farres about her favorite food. But Rida didn't want to leave the two alone.
Enraged she pounced on Ina, caught her by the wrist try-ing to pull her away from Farres.
'Get out of this planet!' she gasped. Ina wanted to cling to the table, missed it and fell down from her chair. Then Farres rushed toward the young women, pushed Rida away and helped Ina to stand up.
'Are you all right?'
Ina nodded, but it was obvious that her whole body was trembling.
'That was just the beginning', Rida screamed. 'I'll make sure that this woman will get out of here.'
'Do you seriously believe, I'd come back to you then?' Farres replied furiously while he was tenderly hugging Ina trying to calm her down.
'Surely you will. You are just confused now.'
'If you attack Ina again, I'll ensure that you will be exiled from Sathorja', Farres shouted at his ex-girl fiend. Then he put some luminous chips on the table to pay for the meal and left the place of the incident with Ina.
'What happened just now?' A voice behind them was as-king. Ina and Farres had walked just 50 feet away when Alons stopped them.
'Please, leave us alone', said Farres panting.

He turned to Ina and said: 'This is my annoying brother Alons.'
'Hallo', Ina said and shook his hand.
Wow, there was a close resemblance between the two. Alons was as attractive as his younger brother and had the same dark eyes. However, he had dark brown hair and he looked rather scruffy. 'This doesn't look too good, Ina', he said and pointed to Ina's reddened wrist. Rida's long finger nails had bored into her skin and left bloody marks.
'Maybe you should visit Liess. She has a tincture that makes these scratches disappear.'
'We wanted to go and see her anyway', Farres replied impatiently. He had imagined the time with Ina in a different way. How could he save the day? The first date had gone terribly wrong.
'By the way, why are you here?' Farres asked his brother, as he didn't show intentions to leave.
'Well, I heard the argument with your ex and wanted to see if everything was okay.'
'And how could you know?' Farres asked intrigued.
'My dear little brother! I hope you remember our silly, but ubiquitous and total surveillance. The whole place is full of cameras, robots, and there's the protocol. You are in a public area, so you are never alone even if you want to.' Alons smirked at Farres.
'Oh no!'
At this very moment Farres began to worry. He had threatened Rida and pushed her away from Ina. Everybody could see the recordings of those ugly scenes. Ina was without rights, and according to the law there was no reason to defend her. Rida's parents might create problems simply because he had the nerve to leave their beloved daughter! And now that row!
'Don't worry! It's good that there's a recording. Xio and also Ronok should see it.'

'What do you expect to achieve by this?' Farres asked doubtfully. 'Both will withdraw the permission they granted us to meet.'
'That's nonsense! The old gentlemen will take care that nothing happens to your amphibious girl.'
'Don't ever talk like this about Ina!' Farres cast a furious glance at his brother.
'Did I say something wrong?' Alons asked with an innocent expression. 'You can't stand the truth.'
'No, but her name is Ina; also for you!' Farres hissed at him.
'That's okay', Alons said placating. 'Pardon me, Ina. I didn't want to hurt you.' Alons extended his hand and said: 'Nice to meet you. Welcome in our family. Our parents expect to meet you soon.' he said with an impish grin.
'At last', Farres said when Alons had gone. 'He can be a nuisance.'
First it was Rida, then Alons. Ina noticed that the entire situation began to overstrain her. Shouldn't she be afraid? Would Rida really do her harm? She looked at her wrist which was gradually turning blue. She had sensed the young woman's hatred; how far would she go?
'I'm very sorry that everything went completely wrong', murmured Farres. 'We'll go and see Liess. She should have a look at your arm.'

Ina walked beside her friend without a word. They were slowly wandering along one of the crowded shopping promenades passing by the oddest shops and boutiques. An ice-cold shudder ran down Ina's back, when she looked at a window display with accessories and spare pieces for robots. Loose heads looking as if they were human stared at her with empty eyes. Extremities hung from the ceiling protruding into the shop window. A trunk stood brightly illuminated in the center.
'We have to go on', Farres said tenderly laying his hand on Ina's shoulders.
'That's weird', she said and turned away gratefully.
A three-story clothes shop attracted Ina's attention. Its display was full up with the most wonderful clothes Ina had ever seen. But Farres pulled her quickly past the shop.
'I want to have a look at the clothes', Ina said angrily.
'Ina, this boutique belongs to Rida's parents. Let's get away from here!'
Ina followed her friend and contented herself with viewing the shops, while they were passing by. This shopping arcade had a particular attraction. It looked like a small town amidst a building. Wells, benches, tables, trees, flower beds, and bushes surrounded by business lines up to five stories high. High up there was a huge arc-like construction made from Ips collecting the sun light to illuminate the gigantic room up to the last corner. A group of school children crossed the way of the young couple.
'Hey, that's the terrestrial woman called Ina', a small boy

shouted. 'My Mom told me about her. She's going to save my aunt.'
'Your grandpa has converted her into a fish, hasn't he?' A little girl with long, brunette braids said.
'Yeah, that's brilliant!' said the boy with bright eyes.
'Silence, kids!' a female voice called out.
Meanwhile Ina, surrounded by kids, noticed with dismay that the alleged caregiver was a robot.
And the children were human? Well, in any case Ronok's grandchild was!
'Don't brag so, Gob!' another girl screamed.
'But it is true' said the boy in his defense and rose a threatening fist.
'Would you like to go swimming with me?' a pale faced kid asked touching Ina's arm.
Ina looked down into two friendly, curious children's eyes.
'With pleasure', Ina replied in an unaccented voice.
'Hey, you have to dive with me as well!' a boy requested.
'Pardon me', said Farres, 'but we have to go!'
'But I want to listen to some stories from Earth', shouted a girl in the crowd. 'They eat animals there, don't they?'
'Yuck!' her girlfriend made as if she had to vomit instantaneously.
'Ok, that's enough, my dear!' exclaimed the robot lady. 'Please, let Farres and Ina go.'
Obediently the kids opened up and gave way.
'Fare well, Ina', Gob called after her. 'See you at my grandparents' house.'
Surely not, Ina thought.
'My goodness', said Ina sighing, when they finally had left the crowded street and came down the stairs again. 'How can they know me?'
'You are famous', replied Farres. 'When you were brought here three months ago, people were upset. To bring you to Sathorja cost a lot of tax money, and then the only reason was Sesa's loneliness.'

Ina looked at her friend for a long time.
'Forget it', Farres said quickly. 'Meanwhile many Sathorjans have a particular sympathy for you.'
'Should I be happy about it?' Ina asked insecurely.
'Of course you should', Farres replied, embraced her under a sudden impulse and kissed her.
They stood there for a long time – they didn't know how long. Eventually they continued their trip through the palace.
'Where are we going?'
'Well, first of all we'll have to go and see Liess', Farres said. 'She is all-knowing, and I'm sure she has the right tincture for your arm.'
'It doesn't hurt anymore, Farres. That's nothing!'
'Maybe, but Liess shall decide, whether a treatment for the injury is necessary or not. Come on, you'll like it there.'
Ina followed her friend walking down a small hidden stairway between two mighty flowerpots. When they went down the stairs, she felt a slight breeze and a strange fragrance.
'Is this the basement?' Ina asked in astonishment. They were passing through a broad, scarcely illuminated corridor. Sparkling, self-illuminating tiles created a magic effect.
''That's the first of three basement stories.'
'Pardon me?' Ina said irritated.
'The building is huge, darling.'
'I know', Ina said panting. 'But the way down here isn't used much. So far we haven't seen anybody.'
'Oh yes, Sathorjans love sun light and open spaces. Most of them have not a very good feeling walking though badly lighted trails. You'll only meet robots.'
'What?' Precisely at this moment half a dozen ball robots rushed towards them. Ina instinctively ducked down. When Farres wanted to go on, suddenly an elegantly dressed, slender, dark haired woman stood right in front

of them. Where did she come from? Ina should have noticed her.
'Nice to meet you', she said with a gentle voice.
Ina looked at her in surprise. She had a well-proportioned face, her blue-green eyes shining forth under long eyelashes. The Bordeaux red costume highlighted her great figure.
'Hi', Farres greeted the red lady. 'Are you on your inspection round?'
'As you know, I'm always busy. I don't need any rest phases, just service units.'
'Pardon me, darling. May I present: This is Tunia. She's a TFR.
'Hallo', Ina said insecurely. What did the abbreviation TFR mean? And what was the meaning of service units? What did she do here in a corridor usually only used by robots?
'Don't be afraid', Tunia began to say gently. Her voice had a soothing effect, as had her charisma. Ina didn't understand exactly why. 'I am a transformation robot.'
'You are what?' Ina stuttered. Incredible; this delicate woman claimed to be a robot. But Farres' next statement capped everything:
'Tunia is a sophisticated combat machine.'
'But…' Ina cast her friend a contemptuous gaze. Was he kidding? This was not funny at all.
'I can transform myself, change my shape', the lady explained patiently. 'I hopefully never get into the situation to show you my true form.'
Ina stared at her with amazement.
'Ina, the TFRs serve as our security. They only interfere when there are problems.'
'Serious problems', remarked Tunia.
'How many TFRs are working here?' Ina asked with a dry throat.
'Six', Tunia answered. A moment later she went on: 'Ina, my equals and I are not dangerous at all. You don't have

to be afraid. We are machines, not humans acting determined by emotions like Rida and Ronok.'
At last Ina achieved to look away from the woman. When she looked up again, Tunia had disappeared as quickly as she had turned up.
'Are you all right, Ina?' Farres asked insecurely.
Ina nodded, lost in thoughts. She walked along with her friend without a word. They went down another staircase and a small corridor which widened and brightened slowly. Then it met with other corridors with had crystal ceilings illuminating the place. Ball robots and humanoid machines crossed the young couples' way, but Ina didn't pay attention to them anymore. Again and again she had to think of Tunia. She had been so nice and patient. It seemed absurd and ridiculous to assume she was a highly sophisticated combat machine.
'That's the kitchen', Farres suddenly said when they entered a large hall. Ina looked around and could see nothing but robots. Lots of robots, old fashioned compared to the TFR. They were primitive and just useful for kitchen work.
'Hallo, Farres and Ina', said a rattling voice coming from a floating object without legs. A head, a body, and long arms made of a dull, red colored material carelessly put together.
Ina observed the machine suspiciously. It had two objectives in the place where the eyes should be. It didn't need a mouth; there were only some tiny holes for the loudspeaker.
'Would you like something to eat or to drink?'
'No, Liess is expecting us.'
'That's all right!' Slowly and silently the robot floated aside and rose up to the ceiling.
'What was that?' Ina asked. Her palms were damp and cold.
'It's a reception robot of the old generation.'

'What else do I have to expect?' Ina asked gasping wiping her hands with her gown.
'I don't know', said Farres grinning. 'Maybe we'll meet some frightening aliens.'
Ina shook her head angrily as she followed Fars through the kitchen. It was strange; they were passing through a kitchen, but there was not the slightest smell of the food prepared here. The kitchen was absolutely sterile; it looked more like a hypermodern factory with its countless machines. There were no pots on hot plates, no dishes or cupboards – nothing.
A group of ball robots whizzed towards them. They were loaded with delicious food. 'They're delivering an order', Farres explained shrugging. 'Soon it'll get very busy here. It's time for the afternoon snack.' When he saw Ina's questioning look, he added: 'I'm sure Liess will have something for us.' Farres lead Ina towards a broad gate, and behind there was another brightly tiled corridor. The surroundings turned more homely and comfortable. Plants were climbing up toward the sunlight entering through glass openings in the ceiling. Ina looked up with surprise gazing directly into the blue sky. How was this possible? She supposed they were in the second or even in the third basement floor.
'Farres, how can there be daylight down here?'
'It's directed here'
'How?' Ina asked.
'The sunlight is captured and focused by large collectors and brought to the deepest floor by means of computer technique.'
'And it's done without mirrors?'
'Hey, you are on Sathorja and not on Earth.'

There was a low chirping; Farres had a short look at his CC3 and said: 'We have to see Shora.'
'What?' Ina asked with surprise. 'She would like to see you and we are quite near her room.'
'Are we?'
'Yes, she has been temporarily placed there.' Farres pointed to a door leading into a room bathed in light. 'Anyway, Liess is with her just now. That's quite convenient.'
'Why does Shora have to live down here?'
'She needs a sterile room and to be near our herbalist. Just wait a second. We'll be picked up by a robot.'
'Not again!' Ina said gasping. She'd had enough of these tin fellows.
A small luminous cube rushed toward them floating a couple of seconds in front of them. Then it went out of their way and buzzed: 'Entrance granted!'
'What does that mean?' Ina asked looking utterly aghast.
'We have just been cleaned' Farres said with a wry smile.
'How can this work?' Ina shook her head panting. Everything was getting too much for her. How could she ever manage to live in this world? They had robots everywhere; part of them looking like humans or having strange functions and working areas like this floating cube.
'Come here', whispered the old herbalist woman and got up ponderously from her wing back chair. Ina was very pleased to see her; she had helped her a lot during the time she had been at the laboratory. Ina's glance fell on the bed in the middle of the room. A pale and delicate figure was lying there. Long, whitish blonde, strawy hair

framed the narrow face white as a sheet. Shora's skin on her hands and arms seemed to be completely transparent. As Ina stared at her, it looked as if her life was fading away. Shora's body was severely emaciated, her cheek bones were standing out, and her lips were thin and white.

'What's wrong with her?' Ina whispered almost inaudibly.

'A serious illness, my love', replied Liess. 'At the moment it's particularly bad. She can't keep anything in her stomach, has high fever, and …' The old lady stopped; she looked at Shora, sighing silently.

'Well, she needs strong pain killers to be able to endure her current state. Her body is disintegrating; it is attacked by a rare strain of virus in her blood. No medicament has been able to cure her.' Liess paused and turned to Ina. 'You are her last and only hope, my darling. The fruits from the Loki Lake are unique and can save Shora. Unfortunately my supplies will be running down soon. We suppose that there are plants in the rift between the hot springs whose fruits are even more powerful than the ones we could get so far, and they might well be able to cure her.'

Ina cast a disheartened look at the old lady.

'You can do it, my child', Liess said with a confident smile on her furrowed face. Then she added seriously: 'There's not much time left. Maybe you should try your luck in the lake during the next week.'

'Ina', a husky voice sighed arduously. Shora had opened her eyes and was staring at her. 'Come here', she gasped. Insecurely Ina turned to the young woman.

'Please help me', she croaked almost inaudibly. Forget my …' Shora had to pause and breathe a few times to be able to go on. '…father. I – have – kids. Please save me', she repeated. A tear rolled down over her pale cheek.

Ina's own worries seemed small now! She felt deeply sorry for that woman. Of course she would do everything

she could to relieve her terrible pain.
Ina nodded and whispered: 'Of course:'
'Thank you', Shora said panting and closed her eyes.
'Ok, my dear', Liess said after a minute of silence. Let's go to my herb kitchen, so I can take care of your arm, Ina.'
'What? Oh yes!' Ina had completely forgotten about Rida's rampage. It simply was ridiculous and not worthwhile thinking.
Farres hadn't said a word; he silently followed Liess and Ina through the bright corridor to the old lady's private rooms.
'Welcome to my world', said the Sathorjan with an inviting gesture. Ina looked around with amazement. She had never seen such a great variety of plants. Multi-colored blossoms in all forms and varieties were filling the room with wonderful fragrances. As Ina walked through the jungle of plants, she saw niches filled up with shelves. There were strange containers filled with many different substances. She stopped with amazement looking at a glass containing five little pulsating spheres of pink color.
'These are the last Gaia-fruits from the lake', Liess said. Carefully she took the container and opened it taking out one of the spheres and putting it into Ina's hands.
'This fruit comes from the edge of the rift. Take a careful look at it. Its healing power is sufficient for many illnesses, but unfortunately not for Shora. The deeper you dive, the better the harvest. Do you understand?'
Ina nodded and gave her back the strange sphere.
'Now sit down with Farres. It's time for you to eat something and to change your Quados.' Liess winked at Ina. At that very moment Ina's CC3 began to make a buzzing noise.
'Oh', Ina said with surprise, 'I completely forgot.'
'That's why we have them. You can't imagine how many things I would forget without it', Liess explained. 'Over there you'll find the Quados. They had the precaution to bring them here.'

Ina slipped behind one of the big, dense plants and quickly changed her Quados. The alarm stopped immediately. Then she sat down beside her friend. The air was filled with a delicious fragrance. A ball robot brought several flower dishes on a small floating table. For Ina there was a mandatory giant glass of water and for Farres a sort of tea.
'Well, let me see, what our Rida has done to you', said Liess and took Ina's arm in her scraggy hands.
'It's nothing', she murmured, while she stood up ponderously and scuffled to one of the shelves.
Ina gave Farres a quick look. He appeared to be pensive.
'Farres?' Ina asked doubtfully. 'What's wrong?'
'The young Sathorjan turned to his girlfriend and said: 'There's nothing wrong, Ina.'
'Just don't move. I'll apply this extract on your arm. It'll make the marks of Rida's nails disappear.'
Liess dribbled a viscous, violet liquid on Ina's arm rubbing it in with a dark blue velvety, leaf.
'It'll hurt a little bit; that's normal, Ina', said the old lady and got up to put away her utensils.
'It doesn't hurt', Ina lied. Before she had hardly noticed the injury, but now?
'Farres, could you please apply Ina the salve. You already know which one.'
'Yes, I will', replied Farres and took a transparent, small container from one of the shelves. Cautiously he applied a creamy substance on Ina's reddened arm.
'It'll get better soon. Liess' treatments are not very enjoyable.'
'You're exaggerating!' commented Liess indulgently.
'I speak from experience. Do you remember, Liess when I was here because of that insignificant injury?'
'Yes, of course, my dear', the old lady replied. 'But you have to admit that my treatments are very effective.'
Farres nodded, cleaned his hand with a cloth and put the container back onto the shelf.

'Thank you', Ina said and had another portion of the wonderful flower dish.
'What else are you doing today?' Liess asked.
'I wanted to show 'Water world' to Ina and go swimming, but I'm afraid it's getting late. We'll put it off till tomorrow.'
Going swimming with Farres? Ina swallowed.
'Oh, that's a wonderful excursion. The water in the orange basin is marvelous and you can relax very well', Liess raved. 'I should also have a break.'
'Do you have a lot of work because of Shora?' Farres asked compassionately.
'Not only because of her. Medicine is always needed, and I still haven't found any skilled assistants. You can forget the robots. I just can't get along with them.'
Ina could understand her very well…
'Did Sesa talk to you about your parents?' Liess suddenly asked.
'I only know that they're alive', Ina said feeling unpleasantly touched.
'Yes, they live on Glosua, an inhospitable planet. I am in contact with them, and they have been asking for you. Is there anything you want me to tell them?'
Ina felt as if she was communicating with afterlife. 'I can't really remember them. When I lost them, I just was a small child.'
'Your mother Elsa is longing for you and Sesa. She is very lonesome suffering severely from remorse.'
Ina looked at her hands unable to say a word.
'You know, your sister deeply wishes to travel to Glosua.'
'Oh, does she?' Ina asked. After a long pause she said in a low voice: 'I have thought for many years that all my family was dead, Liess. My parents left me all alone on Earth. I…' Ina wiped her tears off the corner of the eye.
'That's all right, my dear. Forgive an old woman when she's talking too much.'
Again it became quiet in the herbal kitchen.

'We don't want to detain you any longer. Shora will doubtlessly need your help.'
'Yes, that's true.' Liess took a quick look at her CC3. 'Ronok will visit his daughter soon.'
Then it's time to leave, Ina thought.
'Is Kun still visiting his wife or did he already fall into despair?' Farres asked curiously.
'Oh, I think today he'll turn up again. Shora's brother and sister are also coming, as far as I heard. I suppose, Maris is already with her.'
Ina got dizzy when she mentioned so many people.
'Pardon me, Liess!' Maris asked all of a sudden. She was standing in the door frame having a short look at Ina and Farres.
'Yes?'
'Where's Shora's new medicine?'
'Oh yes, I've put it over there.' Liess pointed to a small bottle filled with a transparent substance.
'Wonderful', Maris said when the old lady gave her the bottle.
'Maris?'
'Yes, Ina.' Maris stopped for a moment looking at the terrestrial girl.
'I'm very sorry for your daughter', Ina stammered. 'Of course I'll do everything I can to help her. I mean I'll try to…' Ina broke off.
'That's good, Ina. Thank you.' Maris turned around and went back to Shora.
'Let's go, darling!'
'Yes.'

The next day Ina just couldn't wait to see Farres. Although she didn't feel like going swimming with him, she longed to see him. Unfortunately he had sent her a message saying he wouldn't have time to see her until late afternoon.

Disenchanted Ina sat down in front of the panorama window and looked out. She loved nature; it calmed her down. This had always been like this…Ina had always loved to be outdoors in the open air since her early childhood. She needed fresh air, the smell of wet earth and flowers, the tickle of blades of grass under her feet, and singing birds at dusk during balmy summer nights. Within the palace Ina had been exclusively in closed rooms for weeks, and that was affecting her good mood.

'Hallo, Ina. Any plans for today?' Sesa asked over the CC3.

'Hallo, Sesa!' Ina replied sighing. 'Not before five in the afternoon.

'You are meeting Farres again, aren't you? What about yesterday?'

'Do we really have to talk this over our computers?' Ina argued annoyed.

'No, I'm coming to see you at twelve and we have lunch together, ok?'

'Why so late? Now it's only half past eight!' Ina wondered. She thought, Sesa had always time and absolutely nothing to do.

'I have to study, Ina', Sesa said panting. 'I missed my last exam in alien life forms and I have to make up for it within three days.'

'What do you need that for?'
'No idea', replied Sesa.
'I have to keep going to that stupid school for another year, until I can finally do what I want.'
'And that is?' Ina asked curiously.
'I'm going to stay with our parents.'
'What?'
'You are also coming, and like this we are a family again.'
'Are you crazy?'
Sesa interrupted the call. Ina looked at her CC3 thoughtfully. Sesa obviously didn't know how lucky she was with her adoptive parents. Why didn't she want to stay? What did she expect from her biological parents? She didn't even know them!

When she came to see Ina, Sesa ignored her completely. She leaned against the door frame and waited without saying a word.
'I'll never move to Glosua', Ina remarked annoyed.
'Perhaps you won't, but I will', Sesa said furiously. 'Come on now, I'm hungry.'
'I'm ready. Where are we going?'
'We are visiting some friends of mine.'
'Pardon me?' Ina asked. – 'Well, I've got some more social contacts. Don't they have this on Earth? There's not much I can do with you. You just like to be with Farres and…'
'That was yesterday.'
'And also the day before yesterday.'
'He visited me at the laboratory. I didn't even know he would come.'
'And today you'll see him again. I wanted to be with my sister, not with an egoist fallen in love.'
Ina suddenly stopped, pressed her hands into her hips staring furiously at Sesa.
'I'm very sorry, because I have so little time for you. I have foolishly fallen in love after I had been kidnapped

and became a mad doctor's victim!' Sesa looked at Ina for a long time; then she eventually said: 'Come on, please!'
A transport robot brought the two girls to the first basement floor.
'Where are we?' Ina asked. The somber light and the strange characters spooking around frightened her. 'Why is it so dim in here?' Ina asked while she was walking behind her sister.
'Some people don't like to sit in the sun all day', Sesa replied.
A filthy room filled with sofas, young people and garish tones – presumably music. Ina felt as if she were in a pub on Earth. Where was the shiny ideal world? Ina looked around. There were neither robots nor aliens, only humans.
'Why did you bring her?' a young man asked. His long hair was hanging shaggily over his shoulders. 'Ina is my sister', Sesa said shortly.
'She is not one of us,' a woman a little older than Ina noted observing the terrestrial suspiciously.
'Oh, Ina', somebody called out. 'Wow, what a surprise!' Tana, a sixteen year old girl, rushed towards the sisters, first embracing Sesa exuberantly and then Ina.
'That's my best friend Tana', Sesa explained visibly relieved. 'And that', Sesa pointed to a white blonde young woman, 'is Zera, her sister.'
'Come and sit down with us', said Zera.
Ina sat down gratefully. She didn't want to attract too much attention. She was glad to be able to disappear in the crowd.
There were two young men sitting at their table. One of them was really nervous; his eyes were constantly wandering up and down. The other one didn't stop talking, and he always had something more to announce. It was annoying.
'Ina, take some of this!' Zera invited. 'There's enough. We've made it ourselves.'

Ina looked at the pie in the middle of the table. Should she try this strange thing? The black mass didn't look very appetizing. But Sesa bottled up that mass as if it were the best food in the world. Merely out of courtesy Ina also had some, and lo and behold that food was delicious.
'It's excellent', Ina recognized.
'My pleasure', replied Zera.
But Ina didn't really want to know, how this food was prepared.
'What job have you been assigned to?' Tana asked while eating noisily.
'I don't know', Ina said confused.
'Well, what was your job on Earth?' she kept asking.
'I have been a commercial clerk; I mean I sold things.'
Ina's eyes had got used to the twilight and she could see everything very well now; also Tana who was looking at her with her dark eyes.
'What sort of things?'
'I sold books.'
'I have heard about it', said the girl thoughtfully. Her round face framed by straggly, jet-black hair looked absent minded. 'Well', she said a minute later, 'we don't have such things.'
'Ina probably will be assigned to water monitoring', commented Zera.
'Well, I was told that they didn't know if she is suitably qualified for this', explained the 'know-it-all'. 'When my kid is in the water, I would like…'
'Well, well', said a deep voice behind Ina. 'You must be the fish girl from Earth who our dear Sesa had to drag to Sathorja by all means.'
A tall man, not much older than twenty five, was pensively observing Ina.
'And how do you like it here?' he asked.
Ina darted a short glance at him and stammered: 'Quite well.'
'Only?' he shouted enraged. 'You are on the most won-

derful planet of this solar system, moreover in the presidential palace and you just say: Quite well. Perhaps your planet is nicer, better, or more livable? Isn't it true that there are wars all the time? Haven't you nearly destroyed the climate and the diversity of species apart from producing vast amounts of waste?'
What did that guy want from her? Seeking for help she looked over to Sesa; however, Sesa herself looked completely surprised.
'Viruses, bacteria, waste, and poison – That's your planet Earth.'
'Shut up, Mogo!' Zera said insistently. 'Ina loves her home planet and that's quite normal. Soon Sathorja will be more beautiful for her, but this will take time. She doesn't know much about our planet yet, don't you Ina?'
Ina nodded.
'Ask us questions', Tana encouraged her.
Ina kept quiet for some time; then she asked: 'Why do you eat purely vegetarian food here?'
'Strange question', Mogo murmured shaking his head. He turned to a noisy group of men and began to talk to them.
Ina was happy that Mogo had lost his interest in her opinion. Apparently he was a patriot, and Sathorja was the most important thing in his life…
'There is a tremendous diversity of plants. The vegetation provides everything necessary for humans, aliens and animals. Therefore we don't eat animal products. That would be a barbarity for us.'
'There are only herbivores on this planet?'
'Yes.'
Ina thought for a moment; then she asked: 'How did life arise here?' She had become increasingly interested, and this was her chance to get the answer to many questions.
'Not on Sathorja. The water planet Wona is thought to be the cradle of creation', commented the 'know-it-all. 'Sathorja is just one of its moons.'

'Is it?'
'In the beginning it was just a deserted chunk of rock. However, there was water and an atmosphere', explained the young man. His blonde hair covered his violet eyes persistently staring at Ina.
'Millenniums ago Sathorja became what it is today.'
'We could say nature was flown in from Wona as well as humans and animals. Plants and animals were especially bred, every species, every flowering plant, simply everything', Zera said firmly.
'But that's impossible!' Ina cried with surprise.
'Nothing is impossible in thousands of years', commented Tana.
'That's a lunacy', Ina gasped. 'Are there anymore moons with an atmosphere?'
'Yes, but most of them are not as cozy as Sathorja. Most money was invested in this planet. It's something like a showpiece.'
Ina paused and emptied her glass.
'I have another question. Do you have something like a religion?'
'We have what?' asked Zera.
'Do you believe in something superior?'
'I don't understand you', Zera replied thoughtfully.
'Well, you must have thought about where you come from and where you go after death. Or why does your Wona exist?'
'Oh yes, I understand what you mean', the 'know-it-all' said sighing. 'Here everybody makes his own world view.'
'So you don't think there's a superior being who created all this?'
'You mean a god?' Tana asked.
'Yes.'
'Some of us do, but only very few. We think, we live and then we die. That's all.'

Ina swallowed. So they were atheists. What would she have done without her religion? How could she be strong enough to cope with all the absurd things that had happened to her? No, she would never give up her faith! She needed it as her elixir of life.
'What about your children? Is there a school system?' Ina wanted to know.
'Of course there is. Children go to school when they are five years old. They are taught exclusively by humanoid robots. They know better how to handle children, have no emotions, and they are fairer', replied the nervous guy at the table.
'How long do they have to go to school?'
'Fourteen years.'
Ina looked at the young man with surprise and murmured: 'In my home country it's only nine years.'
'You can't compare that', reasoned the 'know-it-all'. 'One year on your planet is longer, the calendars don't match.'
'Yes, that's true', said Tana.
'Do you have any celebrations like birthdays for example?'
'Yes, of course Ina!' Tana said smiling. 'Otherwise we would forget how old we are.'
'However, everybody authorized can consult your CC3 and find out your age to the second', Zera commented.
'As all the other personal data', said Tana panting.
Ina knew exactly what that meant. Thoughtfully she looked at her glittering bracelet. They could control everything she did. She better didn't think of it or she would get mad. Total surveillance was impertinence and a violation of human rights! At the moment these rights did not apply to her anyway… Somehow she began to doubt that she was a human being anymore…
'Your technique is very restrictive', Ina commented.
'But on Earth this development has started as well', Zera pointed out.

'Well, but we haven't got so far yet.' Ina had to think of her iPhone she had taken along everywhere, constantly connected to the Internet. Wasn't it comparable to a CC3? These devices were quickly progressing, and the computers were getting more and more powerful.
Lost in thoughts she looked at the glass of water in front of her and said: 'The robots save you a great deal of work. They even teach your children.'
'Oh yes', confirmed Tana. 'Robots are used for lots of tasks such as defense, medical care, and household chores. We couldn't even imagine life without them. Also the infirmary and geriatric care is mainly done by robots.' Ina swallowed.
'I have been at the laboratory, but I never saw any robots', she said thoughtfully.
'Oh, Ronok likes to work himself, and his team is primarily composed of people. He only uses robots for emergencies and doesn't appreciate them. He thinks they make mistakes just like people.'
'It must have been hard for you, Ina?' Zera asked compassionately.
Ina nodded thoughtfully. Somehow she eventually wished she could leave this somber and noisy room.
'Ina, you must not tell my parents anything about all this!' Sesa suddenly said.
'But they will know anyway', Ina said with a fleeting glance on Sesa's CC3.
'It's not a secret, where we are, but they mustn't know what we're talking about.'
Ina looked at her in astonishment.
'Ina, this is – how shall I put it – illegal. The food and the drinks we had are forbidden.'
'What? Are you taking drugs?' Ina exclaimed appalled. She stared at the black pie on the table.
'Who said that?' somebody shouted.
'The terrestrial woman', somebody else replied.
Quickly a circle formed around Ina.

'We don't take drugs', a middle aged, bearded man grumbled. 'Not the way you think, earthling.'
'She's an intruder and will betray us!' an excited voice shouted.
'Oh no', Zera said firmly. 'Ina has questions and is looking for answers. Consider her history.'
'We all know about her', a scraggy, hollow-cheeked woman said. 'Zera is right. Ina is a misfit in society just like all of us.'
'Sesa, you have to vouch for your sister. We don`t need any more problems, otherwise we'd be relegated from the palace, do you understand?' asked the bearded man.
'Yes', said Sesa.
'That's good!' The man made a sign to the others, and everybody got back to their seats again.
Ina breathed a sigh of relief.
'All of us have problems with the strict immigration laws of the Federation of Planets', explained Zera. 'My sister and I are living for a long time on Sathorja, but we still haven't been able to obtain a work permit. We come from a neighboring moon and have lost all our family. We are allowed to live in the palace, but we're not free. Without work we have no money and cannot build a new life. This happens to many people here. This meeting with like-minded people is our only ray of hope.'
'Are you also without rights?'
'No, that's not the problem', Zera said. 'We have civil rights, but just the most important ones regarding our survival. And that doesn't include earning a living. If they find out that we are doing illegal things, we'll be relegated to Hedoncus.'
'What's that?'
'It's a prison planet', replied the 'know-it-all.
'Something like this exists?' Ina asked astonished.
'All criminals serve their sentence there. There are prisons, institutions for mentally disturbed offenders, and residential communities where they are rehabilitated.'

'They are guarded by Reptides, a mixture of robots and animals', Tana said anxiously. 'They have eight legs; their body is many yards long with a highly sensitive head with venomous antennae.'
'An acquaintance of mine did something wrong and was brought to Hedoncus', said the nervous young man with a frightened look. 'One of the Reptides attacked him.' The man stopped and then he whispered. 'He didn't survive.'
'People say that Reptides have been seen on other worlds apart from Hedoncus as well. They are able to adapt to the environment as they are sophisticated robots, have impenetrable amours, and may be programmed for particular target persons.'
Ina had enough. She didn't want to listen to any more horror stories. 'Sesa, I still have to meet Farres. Could you please bring me to the ground floor?' she asked. 'I don't know this area very well.'
'Yes, ok', Sesa said, stood up and said good bye to her friends. The two young women returned to the light and life of the palace.
'How did you like it?' Sesa asked her sister. 'It was quite interesting, but I'm still hungry. I also eat with my eyes, you know, and that black pie wasn't very appetizing.'
'So you can go out and eat once more with your new friend', Sesa said offended. 'What are you doing today?' she asked after a while.
'Farres insists on showing me the water world. I'm not sure if I should be happy about it.'
'Of course you should! It's wonderful. You'll enjoy the trip.'
'Somebody might see my gills. I don't like it. They are absolutely horrible.'
'Everybody knows you have gills, so it doesn't matter at all. Don't you understand?'
Ina shook her head.
'Here you are!' Sesa said when the transporter stopped in front of Ina's flat.

'Thank you', Ina said quickly.
'Ina, please don't talk to Farres about the last hours! He'll tell his brother everything, and then his brother will tell my father.'
Ina said farewell and saw Sesa disappear behind the next corner.
Punctually Farres came to pick her up at her flat.
'Hallo Ina, how are you doing?' he said good-humored. 'Did you have a rest?'
'Yes.'
'Where did you have lunch?' he asked without giving it much importance while they were strolling along a bright and cheerful corridor.
'I went out with Sesa' was Ina's brief reply.
She was grateful that Farres didn't ask anymore. He began to talk about the neighboring town Rambala. Then he told her about his family. Ina was glad he was talking a lot, as she loved to listen to him. This meant she didn't have to talk much.
'My parents live in the city center. Their flat has a superb view. You'll like it, Ina.'
'What are their names?' Ina asked intrigued.
'My mother's name is Mula and my father's Zed. Furthermore, I have a sister called Kara, and you already know my arrogant elder brother.'
'How do they earn their living?' Ina asked lost in thoughts.
'By now they are living on Alons' and my salaries', replied Farres. 'Before my mother made gowns and my father was specialized on micro technique for machines. But he is not well now, so he had to retire from work.'
'I am sorry!' Ina said.
'Kara is studying medicine and doesn't have any own money. She is living at home with my parents and commutes to university every day.'
'I understand. And what does your brother do?' Ina wished to know.

'He is working in the security department like me, but he's Xio's right hand. He has made a career and invested a lot of time and ambition. It suits him; he loves to give himself airs.'
'Do you think so?' Ina had the impression that Alons was quite ok.
'Sesa made my brother manipulate her CC3, so you two could escape from the laboratory', explained Farres all of a sudden.
'Pardon me? But you said that he…'
'You have to forget about that immediately, Ina.'
'I can't understand that', Ina said. Either you represented the law or you didn't.
'He uses his knowledge to sell free minutes to some people in the palace. Of course nobody must know about his extra business.'
'Then he probably would have to go to Hedoncus', Ina said thoughtlessly. Farres suddenly stopped. 'How do you know about that?'
Ina looked at him conscious of guilt. 'I heard about it', she stammered almost inaudibly, and her cheeks reddened.
'Where have you been with Sesa?' he asked sharply.
'I can't tell you', Ina replied without looking at him. 'Please don't ask me!'
'You've been to one of the meetings in the cellar!' Farres said with a sigh. 'Did you eat that black stuff?'
'I tried it', Ina said uneasily. 'Why do you ask?'
'It's forbidden, and we can only hope that Ronok doesn't find out.'
Ina looked at him without understanding.
'He has arranged a highly sensitive computer system monitoring you and giving alarm at any irregularity. Pardon me, but at times your sister is really naïve. She knows exactly what's going on, yet she makes you eat this disgusting pie.'
'It was delicious', replied Ina.
'You have been eating excretions of living beings, Ina.'

At this very moment Ina got sick. Farres had to accompany her straightaway to a toilet.
'I'm sorry, darling!' he said mercifully when Ina left the restroom at last.
'Why did you tell me that?' Ina asked and her face was deathly pale.
'Don't you care what you're eating?' he said with an innocent smile while he led Ina to one of the seats. Gratefully she sat down on one of the sofas. A ball robot brought a container with water and Farres passed it to Ina.
'Thank you. Maybe later', Ina murmured. She still had a queasy feeling in her stomach. She lay down on a bench. Her head rested in Farres' lap who tenderly brushed her hair out of her face. A chirping sound announced a call on Farres' CC3.
'Oh no', he sighed, 'it's Ronok.'
Couldn't he just leave them alone? She felt a little uneasy.
'You have to bring Ina here at once!' Ronok requested.
Ina sat up and looked horrified at her friend.
'I'm sure that's not necessary. She's already feeling better', he said calmly trying not to show his nervousness.
'You don't know. Before Ina has been in the cellar with Sesa and I have a suspicion.'
Suddenly Ina was feeling hot; her cheeks were glowing. She wasn't sick anymore, she was panicking.
Farres fell silent; he didn't know what to say.
'I have known for a long time what's happening down there. They often call me for emergencies, when some of the young people eat too much of the black stuff.'
'Why didn't you tell Xio and Losos?' Farres asked with surprise.
'That's not my job' Ronok said evasively.
'Isn't it?'
'They would send all these young people to Hedoncus without a trial', replied the doctor.
'And you don't have the heart to do that?' Farres asked astonished.

'Zera's and Tana's parents were good friends of Maris and mine, and I promised them… But why do I tell you? Officially I don't know anything about it, do you understand?'

'Yes, I do', Farres said quickly. He knew that the two sisters had suffered a sad fate since their parents and their three brothers had been killed during a war on a neighboring moon.

'How much of the black stuff did Ina eat?'

'She just tried it', said Farres. 'It was my fault. She got nausea when I told her what it's made of.'

'That's strange. Ina is used to eat animal products from Earth', said Ronok.

But not excretions! What did Ronok think of the Earth? Ina started retching again.

'Anyway; it's good that she vomited and got rid of that revolting stuff', Ronok went on. 'Under these circumstances I don't need to see her. It's important that she doesn't have a large amount of the substance in her blood. I don't think so because she is showing normal blood levels. But please make sure she drinks enough water.'

'Yes, I'll do so', Farres said with relief.

'If the nausea doesn't get better, just bring her here.' Farres cast a meaningful look at Ina. 'Are you showing her the water world?' Ronok asked.

That's what I wanted to', said Farres.

'The water will benefit her', commented the doctor and finished the call.

'Are you getting better?' asked Farres worried about his girlfriend.

'Yes', said Ina and took a couple of sips of water. 'What did Ronok mean when he said, water would benefit me?'

'You'll have to find out yourself', Farres said smirking.

'You know, Farres', Ina began to say; 'I would like to visit your family. I'm also interested in visiting the city. Maybe you could show it to me.'

'Yes Ina, by all means.'

Half an hour later, Farres happily said to Ina:
'At last we have reached our destination. It's wonderful, darling!'
A huge, several stories high gate blocked the access. 'What's your admission code?'
'Three, five, seven, four, nil', Farres replied.
'Farres and Ina; your access is granted.' They entered through a tiny oval opening. Ina was astonished to find herself in a sort of forest, an indoor garden. But where was the swimming pool?
'That's a real jungle here', she said gasping while she was following Farres on a winding path. She had a short look on her CC3 and thought about the time of day. Signs appeared in the air she had never learned, but she could instantly read 19 h 30. It was already late, but Farres still wanted to go swimming with her.
The thicket cleared, and a bathing world showed up leaving Ina breathless. It looked supernatural in the light of the setting suns. Ina had already seen many beautiful things, but this view surpassed everything she'd seen before. A wonderful park was lying in front of her. Gently undulating hill chains invited to laze around, and trees and bushes also formed part of the landscape protecting from curious looks. The basins nestled against the surroundings and appeared almost playful. Curves and roundings seemed to be the key elements. A huge glass roof caused the impression of being at the open air, and a slight breeze still increased this impression.

'Do you see the colored trails leading away from the rondeau?' Farres asked.
Ina nodded casting a questioning look at him.
'They lead to the different pools. So the yellow-orange trail goes to the pool of the same color and the turquoise one to the turquoise-blue pool. The colors also indicate the water temperature. Warm color shades mean from 26 degrees centigrade up to almost 40, and if the trail is of green-blue color, the pool is cooler.
Ina looked at the colorful trails leading to all directions. Some led downhill or uphill, passing through a small forest or entering a tunnel. There was something for every taste.
'Which one would you like to take?' Farres asked. Ina looked at him irresolutely. Did she really want to go swimming? Probably there were too many people who would curiously stare at her or even ask questions.
'Hmm, let's go to the cooler colors. Between about 18 and 25 degrees is appropriate for you and…'
'Farres, I don't want to dive!' Ina said desperately.
'This may still change', said Farres smirking and dragged his girlfriend along the turquoise trail.
'The yellow pool over there looks nice', said Ina, when they had climbed on the highest hill of water world. 'Or perhaps we should go to the orange pool behind the little violet one.' Then Ina pointed to a glittering, curved, and very large pool whose water shone in all shades of red. 'That one is marvelous, Farres, let's go there!'
'Ina, this one has a temperature of more than 30 degrees. If you try to breathe in this one, we'll get the greatest problems.'
'I've got everything under control', Ina stated stubbornly.
'I know you have been adapted to water, darling. You have a profound need for …'
'What are you talking about? I don't feel anything like this. I can also sit on the rim and watch you swimming.'
Farres shook his head. In silence and immersed in

thoughts they climbed down the hill.
People here and there were greeting them, and Farres responded to the greetings with pleasure. All these people were strangers to Ina, so she kept her distance. One of the girls walking around through water world with her boyfriend seemed to be very interested in the planet Earth. She tried to start a conversation with Ina, but Ina didn't want to. Then it turned out that it was Ena, a second cousin of Farres.
'Have you met his family yet?' Ena asked intrigued.
'Only Alons', Ina said.
'Oh', replied Ena.
'It's not so easy, Ena. My parents would like to meet Ina, but she needs a special permit to leave the palace.'
'That's foolish! So why don't Mula and Zed come to the palace?' Ena wished to know.
'At the moment they have no time. My father is not well.'
'Oh, well', Ena thought for a while and brushed with her fingers through her long blonde hair. 'Kara owes me a game. Could you please remind Kara, when you see her, Farres?'
'Yes, I will. It's getting late, Ena. I would like to show Ina the blue lake.'
'Well, then you have to hurry up', Ena said panting. 'Ina, do you like it here?'
'It's divine!'
Ina stood at the banks of a spacious lake and looked dreamily across the reflective surface. Due to the low evening sunlight its blue color looked even more saturated; it had different shades reaching from emerald green to cobalt blue. The artificial lake was edged with stones, but when Ina touched them, they turned out to be soft and velvety. Here and there a water plant grew near the shore.
'How deep is it here', Ina asked curiously. She couldn't imagine how they could have made this indoor lake.
'Well, this one is the deepest basin. I think it's almost seventy feet deep.'

'Wow!'
'Well, we like to dive, and competitions are often held. Once I have been to the lake ground. It's marvelous, and there's a lot to discover. Moreover, it's softly illuminated creating its own atmosphere.'
'So you can dive?' Ina asked with surprise.
'Not as elegantly as you and only with some utensils, but yes, I learned to dive.'
Ina let her eyes wander over the artificial lake. Opposite the place they were standing was a lawn for sunbathing. She heard kids running around and laughing. Oh, they were really untroubled and happy. Some adults were looking after them and exhorting them when necessary. Next to the young couple a group of Sathorjans was swimming their rounds. What a strange swimming style, Ina thought while she was watching them fascinated.
'Well then, let's be brave!' said Farres.
'I don't go swimming with the gown!'
'Oh pardon me; the changing rooms are over there. I have reserved one for you and they've already brought your utensils.'
'Considerate!' Ina mused.
Farres led his friend to a nearby forest; however, a closer look revealed it to be a sophisticated mirror wall. Instantly Ina found her cabin; the cylinder with the Quados was obvious. She quickly changed her clothes, but she hesitated for a moment when she saw herself in the mirror. The gills were not visible because the Quados covered them completely which was good. No, she didn't want to dive and she probably would be able to swim with these strange squares on her sides, wouldn't she?
Seconds later she was with Farres on the shore of the artificial lake and stuck her toe into the fresh water.
'That's too cold for me!' she said shivering.
'It has 23 degrees', Fars stated. Then he took a handful of water and splashed it on her.
'Stop it!'

'Come on!' Farres dived into the water and swam a short distance away from the shore.
'Ina, it's marvelous!' Another shower of water drops rained down on Ina.
'Just wait!' shouted Ina. Making great strides she ran into the lake. A moment later she reached Farres and splattered a torrent of water into his face.
'How do you like it?' Farres asked as they splashed around in the water.
'Wonderful', Ina replied.
They climbed out of the water on the other side of the lake. Ina was happy because her Quados stuck perfectly to her skin.
Farres sat down on a big, flat stone or whatever it was, and Ina did so as well. Slowly the supposed stones yielded under their weight and sank down a few inches.
'What's that?' Ina asked anxiously. 'These are seats adapting to your body. That's the best way to relax. Farres sat back and closed his eyes. Ina looked at the dark blue, mirror-like surface. Meanwhile the suns had set. A rust-brown moon had risen and reflected in the water.
Sathorja was extremely beautiful. Ina's thoughts circled around her new life. Actually it wasn't so bad, was it? She had found somebody she could offer her heart to: Farres. She had a family again and was living in a palace on an incredible world. What more could she ask for? Did she really want to return to Earth? Did she need her best friend Eva? To tell the truth, she didn't even remember how she looked like… Well, Ronok was a terrible guy and somehow Rida also was frightening her, but those were just two people. All the others were friendly and treated her well, although she came from an inferior planet.
'Darling, what do you think?'
'You know Farres, I really like it here. I think I'm happy.'
Farres abruptly sat up. He looked at his friend for a long time, took her in his arms and kissed her.
'Well, well…' a voice said.

Surprised Farres and Ina turned around.
An about thirty year old, corpulent man was standing there smirking at them.
'What's up, Piru? Don't you have to go to see your sister?'
'I'm just on my way to see Shora.'
Shora? Ina looked at the Sathorjan utterly aghast.
'Hallo, Ina! It looks like you're doing really well. Is there anything you want me to tell my parents?' He smirked all over his round face again.
'No, thank you.' Ina stammered tonelessly. She didn't like that guy.
'Well, you're going to save my sister's life, aren't you?' Piru asked while he was staring at Ina. 'You look good, but I doubt that your grace will be sufficient for such a daring venture.'
'Piru, get lost!' Farres got angry.
Ignoring the young man's words, Piru said to the terrestrial girl: 'I'm sure you heard of the hot springs in the rift. A good diver has already lost his life down there, you know? He scalded himself. More than 100 degree hot water sprouts out of the gorges there.'
Appalled Ina stared at Piru.
'You have to be careful so that you don't suffer the same fate. My father thinks it's quite easy and he's risking your life to save Shora's.' Piru shook his head. 'Anyway, it's my sister's own fault. If she had listened to me, she wouldn't have become infected.' He made a dramatic pause and said: 'Don't bother. This is a nice place to snuggle.' He winked at them when he left.
'Piru is a difficult case', Farres said sighing. 'He is, so to say, the black sheep of the family.'
'What did he mean when he said: It is Shora's own fault having caught this disease?'
'I don't know', Farres replied and looked at his CC3. 'It's late. We should swim back.'
'When shall we meet again?' Ina asked disenchanted.

'I can't tell you. I'll have a lot of work during the next days. You'll have to content yourself with Sesa.'
Ina made a fretful face.
'I'll try to come and see you as soon as possible. You have to believe me.'
'Will you present me to your parents?'
'Yes, of course', replied Farres and kissed her again. They crossed over the lake together. Shortly before they arrived on the shore, water world was already deserted, and Ina felt a strong desire to submerge herself.
'Farres, I'd like to stay a little longer. Do you think that's ok?'
'I think so. Sure, I'll have to report.'
'What?'
'There's nobody here anymore. Water world is closed for today. Your CC3 doesn't work under water, so I have to report to security department that you're still here.'
'I understand. Do you mind?' she asked insecurely.
'No, not at all. Will you find your way back to your apartment with the device?'
'I think so.'
You just have to express your wish, and the CC3 will lead you through water world back into your bed.' Farres smirked at Ina.
'That's ok. I know my way home. You were right. I have the desire to dive down; I don't know why.
'That's witchcraft', Farres smiled, kissed his girlfriend good bye, and went to the changing room. When he turned around there wasn't a trace of Ina anymore.

Fascinated Ina dived down the lake. There was a weak blue light illuminating the bottom. Objects of different size and structure rose from the ground emitting their own diffuse light. The bottom was full of sand whirling up when it was touched. Sometimes she saw a small plant full of tiny flowers. Ina decided to ask Sesa about them the next day.

The water suddenly became cooler and she noticed a slight current. That made her curious. Maybe there was an underwater spring. Somehow the lake had to be fed. A little further on, the current became so strong that Ina had to give up. Suddenly she saw a grid. At some distance she could see bars painted in red. There the water was fed into the lake. Slowly she let herself float upwards, reached the surface, and looked around.
Silence was all around; it was almost daunting. The weak lighting around her caused a queasy feeling in her stomach. Shouldn't she better stay in the lake? Nothing much could happen to her. When she went under water, her body automatically switched to gill breathing. Water meant safety and security to her. It was strange. This had been quite different before…
Ina let herself float on the surface and looked up to the stars. Slowly her eyes closed, and she fell asleep for a couple of minutes. The lake simply was too cold to stay in the water. Shivering she returned to the shore. The fresh air did not warm her either. She couldn't find a towel; the changing room was cast into complete darkness. It would have been wiser to go home with Fars instead of being left all alone at the lake. She tried desperately to clear her thoughts staring at her CC3 – for heaven's sake; it was long after midnight. Perhaps she should look for a warmer pool. But if weariness overcame her, wouldn't she drown? Ina was shuddering again. She couldn't stop shivering and huddled together onto one of the strange stones. It felt warm while it was slowly yielding under her weight. Did that funny thing have a heating? Ina cuddled up with it and instantly fell asleep.
'Ina!' Sesa shouted, 'wake up!' Ina stretched out contentedly. Wow, in broad daylight, water world was gorgeous, too. It didn't glitter so much; the sunlight before noon was completely different.
'Where did the blanket come from?' she asked with surprise.

'Maris brought it.'
'Has she been here?' Ina seemed confused.
'She was together with her husband.'
'What? But why?' Horrified Ina stared at her sister. Did she forget her Quados again yesterday?
Ina bit her lips.
'Thanks to Maris this morning you didn't wake up in the laboratory. Ronok was quite indignant', said Sesa. 'There's something I can't understand.'
'What is it?' Ina asked tonelessly.
'Why didn't you wake up with the alarm? Maris told me they found you fast asleep.'
'I have no idea', Ina replied. She could vividly imagine the quarrel between Maris and her husband. Maris was really supporting her, and deserved a thank you – or the saving of her daughter…
'I always hear every little beep from my CC3', Sesa said sighing.
'Last night I was really tired', Ina murmured thoughtfully.
She got up quickly, stretched and went instantly to the changing room. It's good to get dressed and leave water world even though it was very nice…
'Ok, but you like it, don't you?' Sesa asked on the way.
'It's dream-like. Have you ever been diving?'
'Are you joking? We learn to dive when we are children. Everybody can dive; somehow it's a national sport.'
'Oh, I understand', Ina replied.
'Even Liess goes diving from time to time.'
'Incredible!'
Fleet footedly Ina climbed on the waiting transporter. Wherever Sesa would bring her, she didn't care. When the racing journey began, she held on tight and enjoyed the surroundings quickly passing by.
'How is your arm?' Sesa asked.
'It's ok.'
'Rida is completely mad.'

‘That’s right’, Ina said panting.
‘Keen on breakfast?’
‘Oh yes’, Ina said pleased.

Meanwhile Ina knew her way around the palace quite well. Sesa had shown her the shopping streets, water world, the big ballroom, the space port – and the 'dream room'.
Ina was out of breath when they left the space port.
'That was marvelous', Ina said gasping. 'I can't believe how those giant things can fly. They are so huge; our Jumbo jets are tiny compared to them.'
Sesa looked at her with irritation.
'Jumbo jets are big planes on Earth', Ina quickly explained.
'Nice', Sesa said thoughtlessly, 'but I didn't show you the coolest thing yet.'
'What? Can you still surpass this?' Ina said astonished.
'We'll have to walk quite a distance. If we use the transporter, it'll reveal where we've been.'
'The CC3 will do anyway.'
'Yes, we'll go and see Alons. He'll switch off the devices for a moment.'
'What? Are you crazy? Do you really think I want to get problems again?' Ina said annoyed.
'No, if anybody gets problems it's me', Sesa calmed her. 'You just have to see it. I think you'll love it.
Ina stopped for a moment.
'Please Ina. You have to accompany me. I love that room. You can have fantastic dreams.'
'Ok', her sister said with a resigning sigh.
Sesa led her through somber, winding corridors to a dark room.

'What are you doing?' Ina asked when her sister pushed her into the room.
'Alons is coming in a minute.'
'Superb!' Ina commented. She could hardly see a thing in the dark. Why this secretiveness?
Soon she got the answer:
'Mom and Dad don't know about the dream room. The people, who told me about it, want to keep the secret. They use it as a retreat from their stressful lives far away from any surveillance.'
'Well, can everybody simply switch off the CC3s here without anybody noting?' Ina asked surprised.
'Yes', said a cheerful voice behind them. It was Alons.
'There you are at last', Sesa said visibly annoyed. 'Maybe once in a lifetime you could arrive on time!'
'I don't serve you alone, darling', replied Alons. 'Hi, Ina!'
'Hallo', Ina greeted him.
'Well, girls, give me your pretty bracelets.' He took an unsuspicious square-shaped device out of his pocket. Instantly the room was filled up with a strong blue light. Ina did the same thing as Sesa and held her CC3 into the resulting cone of light.
'Is your arm ok again?' he asked.
'Yes, thank you', Ina said.
'Are we ready?' Sesa asked impatiently.
'When you hear the beep, my love.'
A squeaking tone sounded. Instantly Sesa grabbed Ina's arm and pulled her out of the room.
'A thank you would be nice!' Alons shouted after the two women.

'So much ado for such a boring room', Ina grumbled. The dream room was completely white. The sparse equipment wasn't very colorful either. A couple of sofas were standing around uncharitably. There were no plants and interestingly no windows.
'Why did you bring me here?' Ina asked.

'Well, let's start the simulation.'
Suddenly it got dark. Ina lost the orientation. She was on a mountain surrounded by water and in the haze far away she could see land. A breeze carried the fragrance of flowers into her nose. Above her a strange, colorful bird was flying in wide circles letting out strident yells.
The landscape changed, a sunset over a flowering meadow. It was simply precious. But wait a minute; that was on Earth! Just one sun, the flowers, a soft breeze caressing her body – all this was familiar to her. Fleecy clouds made for an even more enchanting picture. Ina took a step forward and then began to run while she felt the long haulms tickling her palms. The scene changed again. She knew that street and the house, too. She had been living there before her family had been legally declared dead. She could hardly remember the fire-red wooden picket fence and the pale green house. Ina's heart grew heavy.
'We were at home then', Sesa said touched. Ina went into the virtual building and sat down on her bed.
'Switch it off', Sesa suddenly said to her sister.
'Please!'
'But…'
'Please!' Ina repeated imploring.
All of a sudden the room turned bright and white again. Ina sat on the sofa hiding her face.
'Don't you want to see Dad and Mom again?' Sesa asked.
Ina looked at her, wiped off the tears and said softly: 'I can't give you an answer to that. My parents are strangers to me as there are to you. Both of us have still been very small, when we lost them, and it's a long time ago.
Ina, they're our Mom and Dad. We could be a family again, you understand?'
'I don't know if I really want to, Sesa.'
'Why not?'
'I'm an adult and I've learnt to live without them. I'm not really prepared to let them get into my life again.'
'Pardon me?'

'They abandoned me, Sesa.'
'But…'
'They took you along, but not me.'
'It looks as if you'll never forgive them.'
'I don't know', Ina said gasping.
The light went out again. Ina was under the water now. She was diving with the Iaos in an incredible depth. Then she suddenly was on land midst a breathtaking splendor of plants. She stood up, pushed some branches aside and discovered a wonderful landscape with rivers and little streams. Ina followed one of the streams and saw myriads of animals; she was fascinated and inebriated so she stopped to inhale the good air into her lungs. From a fountain arose a stream that turned into a river disemboguing into a dark-green lake.
'Wow', Ina stammered. A herd of hairy lizards the size of dogs passed by behind her. And again she heard the yells of the colorful bird flying in circles above her.
'This is a small section of Wona, the water planet. It's important for the water supply of many dry planets.
'All this is drinking water?' Ina asked reverently.
'Yes, sure', said Sesa. Unfortunately this planet has often been the victim of terrorist attacks against the government of my adoptive father. Wona doesn't have any inhabitants because it's quite inhospitable apart from a couple of months in summer. But it's first rate for holidays. Would you like to go?'
'Oh yes. It looks really interesting. Are there monsters?' Ina asked.
'No, the region where we go on holiday is free of beasts on land and in the water.'
Ina looked at the wild and romantic landscape: There were tiny green islands in countless lakes, a wonderful fauna and flora, fascinating countryside as well as rugged rocks and cliffs.
'Is Sathorja so nice, too?' she asked intrigued.
'Oh yes. I mean, the water planet tops it by far, but there's

also a lot to discover here.'
'That's enough for me', Ina said gasping. 'It has given me a lot of impressions. This was great. Thank you.'
'Please don't talk to anybody about the dream room, ok?'
'Does Fars know about it?'
'Sure, also does all his family, Ronok, Maris, and their children. Of course Liess does and many others.'
'So why mustn't we tell Xio and Bora and keep it in secret?'
'The dream room, as its name says, invites us to dream and to forget about our duties. We just devote ourselves to our desire to immerse ourselves into a fictive world.'
'You mean it causes addiction?'
'Yes, but not just that. It may lead to a loss of reality especially in unstable personalities.'
'Oh, I can imagine.'
'Well it also causes dissatisfaction and sadness. All this is just a technical marvel, nothing more.'
'Who has constructed it?'
'I don't know.'
'Hey girls, your time's running out. Please get out there at once!' It was Alons' voice coming loud and clearly out of Sesa's CC3.
'Ok. Thank you, Alons.'
'At last!' The call ended.

The days passed by and Ina missed Farres. Where had he gone? Just being with her sister day after day was boring. A visit to Xio and Bora turned out to be very exhausting, because Sesa was talking endlessly about her biological parents. This bothersome topic hurt Bora so much that she had to leave the room during the meal.

Thereafter Sesa and Xio had a terrible quarrel, and Ina left only to run right into Rida who obviously had been waiting for her.

'Hey, you look out!' screamed the young Sathorjan and swept Ina's wonderful, Bordeaux-red dress over the floor. 'Now it's infested!' she hissed.

Ina darted an angry look at her.

'Am I getting on your nerves?' Rida asked smugly.

'Stop sending stupid messages to my CC3!'

'Wow, you are really brave today, aren't you?' Rida shouted surprised.

She grabbed Ina's arm and yelled: 'You have no idea who you're dealing with, you terrestrial beast!'

Ina stared at her without saying a word.

'My family has great influence, and we are used to get everything we want to have. Farres is my boyfriend, and he'll return to me soon, you understand? I'll make sure that you will be expelled from this planet, you parasite!'

Ina tore away from her and huffed with a quivering voice: 'Farres likes me, Rida, and you can't change it.'

'Yes, for sure I will! Maybe you get astray out there or you have an accident.'

'Surely not with that total surveillance', Ina replied and tried not to show her fear.
'Everything is possible, fish lady! I can fool the technique as I can outwit you, too. I'll tell Ronok to sell you. He hates you and he will be happy to get rid of you.'
'I have to save Shora', Ina replied tonelessly.
'Ha! You'll never achieve that. You think you are a superwoman. That old idiot Ronok will be disappointed with you and flog you to the scientists.'
Ina turned around and tried to keep her composure leaving the slobbering Sathorjan woman with dignity. She wished she could switch off her CC3. The news she had lately got from Rida had been partly frightening, but also embarrassing. Why had Rida to communicate every detail about her past relationship with Farres, telling her every kiss, every display of affection, and so on? Ina actually did not want to know that!
Well, Rida applied a demoralization tactic, and it worked. Ina was insecure and began to have serious doubts about Farres' love.
The same day in the afternoon Ina went to water world. She walked on all the trails, rounded all the pools observing the water in all different color shades. Did she want to dive? Yes, it was time to do so, but was this wonderful pink-violet pool the right one for her? Who could she ask?
Oh yes, her CC3! Well, the pool had 25 degrees, was thirty feet deep, had a tiled floor, and several grottoes. It measured about one hundred by one hundred feet; big enough to be left undisturbed. Today there weren't many people in water world anyway.
When Ina went to the changing cabins, she heard Farres calling her name.
'There you are, Darling!' he said pleased, when he approached her. 'I have been looking for you everywhere!'
'Did you?'
'What a silly question'

'Well, you never come to see me now', Ina said annoyed. 'That's because I have to work', he said equally annoyed. Lately there's something wrong with you', he went on. 'You seem very absent minded.'
Ina looked at him for a moment, and then she turned to the changing cabin.
'Ina, you can't simply go away!' Farres called out. 'I took one day off today, so we can go out together to see some nice places. But if you prefer to go diving…'
'Farres', Ina sighed powerlessly, 'it's not because of you. Rida has been waiting for me again. She…'
'What did she do to you?' Farres wished to know. Ina laid her hand on her forearm which had turned red and swollen. 'She threatened me again. I don't know how to deal with it.'
'I'm going to speak to Xio', Farres concluded.
'Please ask him to block my CC3 for any news from Rida.'
'Pardon me?' Farres asked surprised. 'You didn't tell me anything,'
'How could I? I haven't seen you for two weeks', Ina said angrily.
'But we talked to each other every day', Farres replied. 'What messages does she send you?'
'Just everything about your relationship', Ina whispered.
'I can't believe it!' Farres shouted indignantly. Suddenly he understood why Ina was behaving towards him in such a strange manner.
'Ina', he sighed and embraced his girlfriend. 'I love you, darling. I've never had the same feeling for Rida, not even in the beginning.'
'Nevertheless you have…' Ina stumbled. She wasn't able to pronounce the right words.
'I couldn't resist', Farres replied resigning.
Ina thought of her fiend Eva. She was right saying that men only follow their basic instincts.
'Just forget it. I suppose you've already had a relationship, didn't you? And I don't mind what you did to-

gether.
Ina's cheeks reddened.
'You see?' said Farres smirking and kissed her.
'What about going to Rambala to visit my parents?' he asked a little later.
She stared at him with eyes wide open. 'I'd love to!' A little distraction would be nice.
Farres looked on his CC3. 'Wonderful! The next glider is leaving in half an hour. We can easily reach it.'
'What? Today?' Ina asked with surprise.
'Sure. We'll be at my family's house at about five pm. That's perfect.'
'Ina took her seat on the transport platform. She was a little excited; at last she was allowed to leave this building and enter a strange world, a city. The meeting with Farres' parents evoked a queasy feeling in her. When she last met future parents-in-law, the visit had been a fiasco.
'What do you think, darling? You look so absent minded.'
'Nothing special', Ina murmured.
The flight with the glider was a challenge for Ina. The strict controls she had to undergo gave her a hard time.
'How long will you stay in Rambala?' a beefy robot asked her while a small floating device was buzzing around her.
'A couple of hours', Ina replied trying to keep calm.
'What's your exact address of your usual residence in Rambala?'
Ina turned to Farres seeking help who was waiting for her a few yards away shifting impatiently from one foot to the other. The glider would leave in ten minutes, and Ina was still in the control area.
'I'm traveling with Farres; please ask him.'
'You should have done this before.' After a short silence the robot stepped aside.
'The terrestrial Ina may pass', said the floating and buzzing device suddenly and disappeared.
Unnerved Ina walked over to Farres. 'What was this for?'

'The usual procedure', commented Farres, took her by the hand leading her into a large room. It looked comfortable with sofas, seat groups, plants, and ball robots serving drinks and food. Most of the places were already occupied, but Farres and Ina could still get a seat at the window.
'When does the glider arrive, and how can we get onto it?' Ina wondered while she was looking out of the window.
'We are already on it, darling. This is our plane. In a few seconds the gliding flight will begin. Don't be surprised when you are pressed into your seat. We are gliding very quickly. Rambala is almost one hundred miles away and it'll just take ten minutes to get there.'
'Is that a glider?' Ina asked with astonishment.
'Yes, that's a model from the latest generation. They are prepared for long distance flights. We'll already get out at the first stop.'
'Ina turned around again. Suddenly the glider moved abruptly forward accelerating like a super-fast roller coaster leaving the airport at high speed. Ina tried to sit comfortably, but in vain. The pressure caused by the acceleration was unpleasant. Outside the window the Loki Lake quickly passed by. Only now Ina noticed how big this lake really was. It looked like a small ocean. How could she ever have reached Rambala swimming? Sesa had to be really naïve. Ina shook her head lost in thoughts.
Her eyes wandered all over their compartment again. Humans and aliens of all different kind sat together; some were talking, others dozing. Nobody took offence at anybody; apparently they perfectly understood each other. On Sathorja the peaceful coexistence was not a problem. Why was it so difficult on Earth?
'Rambala', a loudspeaker said.
The glider station in Rambala looked modest. No impressive decoration, no magnificent plants; just a sober hall with green tiles which could be crossed in all directions

by means of conveyer bands. Some of them went slightly upward, others downward, and some rounded sharp corners.
Farres pulled Ina onto an even conveyer. Slowly they passed through a wide, windowless, blue corridor. A group of blue-skinned aliens stood next to them, much too near, as Ina uneasily noticed.
'Hi, you two!' said one yellow eyed human creature with turquoise color skin and hair. You are going to visit somebody, aren't you? Let me guess – his parents.' The creature looked at Farres for a couple of seconds and then it cheered: 'Direct hit! – You're not from Sathorja, aren't you?' the creature asked Ina. Farres made a sign to Ina that they would have to get off the conveyer band to one side.
'Wow, you are that woman from Earth, aren't you?' The other aliens applauded with their blue shimmering hands.
'Sorry, but the show is over', said Farres, held Ina's hand, and took a big step off the band. Ina tripped, but Farres saved her from falling down.
'Killjoys!' the turquoise beings called out while they were transported further on.
'These are Gulins from Tonson, a small planet in the twin sun system. You should not contradict them, otherwise they can get awkward. They have a tendency to read our thoughts and interpret very well our facial expression and gestures. Therefore the Gulin people are quite unpopular on our planets.'
'I understand', replied Ina and stopped reverently. There were in the center of a large oval ground surrounded by large colorful sculptures.
'Welcome in Rambala', Farres said happily. 'This is my home town. I was born and grew up here. As you see, this is a meeting point. These sculptures symbolize the United Planets.'

'Where's Sathorja?' Ina contemplated one artwork after the other.
'It's the bright, yellow-white spiral with the many dots.'
'Hmm, that's interesting.'
'The spiral form indicates that all the important decisions are taken there.'
'Which planet is represented by this orange color disk?'
'That's Quosa, one of the smallest and most inhospitable planets. It's inhabited by a very rare species.'
Farres had a fleeting look on his CC3.
'Well, darling. My parents are expecting us.'
But Ina was staring bewitched at a blue, shimmery oval. Its structure looked blurred before her eyes; it seemed to flow.
'This sculpture represents Wona, the water planet.'
'Sesa told me about Wona', Ina murmured. 'It must be very beautiful.'
A nostalgic desire floated through her body.
'That's true. One day we'll go there for our holiday. I promise.'
Ina nodded. She stopped looking at the wonderful sculptures and followed her friend across the oval. A broad street was 'greened' and lined by high colorful buildings. All the houses had panorama windows, seemed to be built in one piece, and were brightly colored. There were of red, green, neon-yellow, lilac, pink, blue, turquoise, and orange color. Ina couldn't see the roofs; they rose to swindling heights. There were elevators made from glass in front of every building. People went up and down in them. There were no crossroads. Marvelous trees with big, jagged leaves and mighty grey trunks decorated the sidewalks on the left and the right side of the street. Farres had to pull Ina several times of the road to avoid collisions with transporters or other people. Ina was just looking at the houses, while she was staggering like a sleepwalker passing in between the edifices.
The street became even broader leading to another wide

oval. In its center there was a pond surrounded by flowering plants.
'Please don't get silly ideas now!' Farres said smirking.
'Do you think that's funny?' she snarled at him.
'Pardon me!' murmured the young Sathorjan. Ina curiously looked around. No houses, just an oval ground in the middle of nowhere? Ina could see the limits of the oval, but where house were supposed to be, was just nothing. Nevertheless she saw that the people simply vanished as if they were passing through invisible doors.
'What's that?' Ina stammered horrified. 'Where do they go?'
'That's my fault', said Farres. He took her wrist touching for a moment her bracelet. Suddenly they were surrounded by buildings; wonderful houses from glass, shining and glittering in the sunlight.
'But how is that possible?' she asked looking in all directions.
'It's a safety measure for newcomers like you. It's just a trick.'
'Awesome.' Ina simply enjoyed looking at the surroundings. The people they met on their way were dressed in colorful clothes; a feast for the eyes. She herself was wearing a modest, ultramarine gown without any finery. The women she saw were much more elegantly and lavishly dressed. Ina noticed that she was getting a little envious.
'Isn't it fantastic?' Farres asked.
'I don't know what to say', Ina said.
'Maybe you should say you'd finally like to meet my parents?' Farres said smiling.
'Oh yes, of course. I had completely forgotten.'
'They live over there.' Farres pointed at a crystalline building that stood out due to its simpleness. It was higher than the others and looked like a positioned cuboid made from glass.
Thoughtfully Ina looked at the building. 'Which floor do they live in?'

'In the twenty-third floor.'
'Pardon me?' Ina's eyes wandered up the building's wall. 'I hope there's an elevator.'
'Yes, sure there is. You're standing right in front of it.'
Ina jumped backwards staring at a platform on the floor in front of her. She pointed with a trembling finger at the supposed lift.
'Yes, that will take us up', said Farres. He put himself on the platform waiting with growing impatience for his girlfriend to join him.
'I can't do that', Ina stuttered.
'Will you come with me, if I hold you in my arms while we are going up?' asked Farres with an irresistible doggy look.
'We may fall down', Ina gasped.
'That's nonsense! When you come with me, surrounding walls are automatically raised up. You don't seriously think our elevators just consist of platforms without protection?' Farres shook his head and smirked. Ina looked at him with reddened cheeks.
'You can close your eyes while we speed up.'
'Speed up?' Ina asked doubtfully.
'Well, this is a high speed elevator.'
'Oh my God', Ina said and sighed.
'On Earth you also have high buildings with elevators. That's nothing new to you!' Farres said impatiently.
'Not where I come from', Ina groaned.
'My family is waiting.' Farres looked onto his CC3 again. 'Ina!'
'Yes, I'm coming. Ina went a bit shaky toward the platform. She clung to her boyfriend, felt that he hugged her firmly, and the ascent began. The elevator speeded rapidly to lofty heights, until it stopped unexpectedly. Ina kept her eyes closed all the time. Her knees gave in and Farres had to carry her from the elevator to his parents' flat.
'What has happened?' Mula, Farres' mother, asked worried.

'Oh, that's Ina', Farres said with a wry smile. 'The ride in the elevator didn't do her any good. I'll carry her into the living room.'
'Yes, of course', replied Mula.
Ina was terribly embarrassed. She was lying outstretched on the sofa and couldn't even sit up due to the vertigo.
'You'll be ok in a minute, child', said Mula in a motherly tone. 'My first ride in this elevator also was a challenge. Well, a sip of water will surely do you good, hmm?'
Just thinking of it almost made her faint.
'So this is your girlfriend', said an about nineteen year old girl. 'She's looking a bit pale.'
'She's not well', the mother said quickly.
'Was it the ride in the lift?' Kara asked intrigued.
Ina nodded.
'I understand. Hallo, I am Kara, Farres' little sister.'
'Hallo', said Ina gasping while she was trying to sit up. But in the same instant she let herself sink back again. Impossible!
'Haven't you got a medicine for her, Mom?' Kara asked. 'Maybe we should give her the drops I always take.'
'No Kara. Ina is from the planet Earth and she is different.'
'What's going on?' Alons suddenly asked. 'You hardly left the palace and you're already half dead!'
'She's sick, Alons', explained Kara promptly. 'So leave her alone!'
'Farres, you should have reduced the elevator's speed', Alons said lecturing.
'I didn't know that she would react this way', replied Farres apologizing and stroked Ina's hair lovingly.
'You'll get better in a minute', Mula said quickly and put the glass of water on a circular floating table. 'Have some if you are thirsty, Ina.'
'Where's father?' Farres inquired when they had all sat down around Ina.

'He'll come home any minute', Mula replied. 'He had to go to his therapy.'
'Has he still got problems with his joints?' Farres asked.
'Yes, it hasn't improved much', said his mother sighing. 'At nights it still aches.'
'That's bad', Farres said. 'Did he go to see Ronok?'
'No. Ronok's advice is expensive. We don't have so much money', his mother replied lugubrious.
'Ina, you could help our father', Alons said smirking. 'You can always see Ronok and…'
'Shut up', Farres snapped at him. 'Ina is not Ronok's friend.'
'It was just an idea!'
Ina looked from one to the other. Slowly she was getting better. She carefully sat up and grasped the glass of water.
'What a miraculous effect a name can have!' Alons said grinning.
'Alons', his mother exhorted shooting a warning glance in his direction.
Time went by, they had an interesting conversation, and Ina asked a lot of questions. She compared Sathorja with Earth – quite a surprise for Farres' mother.
One hour later, Zed, Farres' father, returned home. He was friendly and charming. He reminded her Farres. There was a strong resemblance. However, Alons resembled his mother. In Kara's case, Ina couldn't tell. In this family Ina felt very well.
When had she last been living in a family? When had she ever felt so much love and caring?
During the wonderful and comfortable meal Ina jauntily began to tell her story. She had a broad smile on her face when she began to talk about her hometown; she answered questions, laughed at jokes, and was happy and content.
It really might have been a nice afternoon and evening…

'What was this phone call just now?' Mula asked with concern, when she noted Alons' look.
'It was Xio', replied her son. 'It's about Shora.'
'And why does he tell you?' Zed wondered.
'Ina has to return immediately. Tomorrow she'll be sent to dive into the rift.'
'What?' Farres asked horrified.
'Shora's getting much worse again. She urgently needs fresh medicine. The fruits Liess had are already too old. They have too little effect.'
'What do you have to do with it?' Kara wondered.
'I have to ensure that Ina immediately returns to the palace. She has to see Ronok.'
Ina got breathless.
'Don't worry, Alons. I shall do that', Farres said quickly.
'I'm sorry, but I have to accompany you. It's my job.'
'No', Ina stammered looking around seeking help.
'You can do it, child.' Mula stood up and hugged Ina like a mother does. Ina started to weep although she tried not to show her feelings.
'Come on, the next glider leaves in fifteen minutes', Alons urged.
'You are cruel', Kara scolded. 'Don't you see how desperate Ina is?'
'I have an order, little sister.'
The good bye was really hard for Ina. Tears kept running across her cheeks.
'You are always welcome', said Zed while saying farewell.

'Thank you', Ina said sobbing. She had the impression that there wouldn't be a next time. The deep rift in the Loki Lake with its hot springs seemed to her like a death sentence.
Without a word she returned to the palace with the brothers. A transporter brought her to the laboratory, where she was promptly received by Maris.
'Thank you very much to both of you', she said and took Ina's hand trying to bring her into the abhorrent room. Ina refused to take a further step forward. Fear and panic gave way to resignation and silent desperation.
'No', she screamed when she saw the machines.
'Ina, you have promised to help Shora', said Maris close to tears. 'My husband won't do you any harm. We just have to talk. Please, come with me. You can sit down next to the window.'
Somehow Maris achieved to maneuver Ina into the lab. Ina obediently took her seat on the sofa, but she was shivering desperately. Liess, Ana, her friend Okon, and Ronok were already expecting her.
For an entire hour they explained her, how she had to get the fruits in the rift. She learned about the unpredictable currents and the dangerous hot springs. Okon extensively explained to her the available technical auxiliaries. There were two diving robots illuminating under water and a transport platform that would wait for Ina and follow her. Furthermore, she had to wear special gloves to pluck the fruits to prevent the healing fruits from burning her hands. And she had a bag to carry the harvested fruit.
Ana's delicate task was it to talk to Ina about her breathing system and to explain, what she needed to be concerned about while diving in the rift. The water temperature was crucial. If the water was too warm, it would damage Ina's gills.
'Ina, that's all I had to say.' Her eyes wandered over to Ronok who nodded toward her. Ana looked at Ina for

a moment and said: 'Please, take the soporific now.' She pointed to a small flask containing a lilac color liquid. Ina stared at it.

'We have to do the function test.'

An ice-cold shudder ran down her spine. Horrified she remembered the long and painful minutes in the lab before.

'Ina, we have no time', Ronok commented angrily. 'It's your choice. If you want, you can also do the test whilst fully conscious.'

'Ina, Ronok won't do you any harm', Liess said grandmotherly. 'Be confident!'

Ina looked at Maris. She was forming a silent 'Please!' with her lips.

'You have one more minute; then I'll instill you the Yso-syrup, you silly thing. I think you remember its effect. I can't risk my daughter's life waiting anymore.' Ronok was standing in front of Ina coldly staring at her.

'Darling!' Maris growled, stood up and gave the flask with soporific to Ina. 'Don't listen to him. He's talking nonsense', she said softly and stroked the young woman's head. Ina looked at Maris' eyes, saw her desperation and swallowed the liquid without a further word.

Ina climbed out of a small glider onto a transport platform that was floating a few inches above the Loki Lake. Two diving robots had been lowered into the water. Ina saw big air bubbles swirling upwards.

'You can do it', Farres called out to her from the loading space of the small glider. He had come to support her together with Ana, her friend Okon and two technicians.

'The robots are positioned above the rift', one of the strangers said. 'Ina!' he called out loudly, 'you can start now.'

Ina nodded, cast a last look at her boyfriend and jumped into the water. She followed the light cones of the robots into the dept. She had a bag over her shoulder, although this prevented her a little from swimming.

The surroundings were bizarre. The steeply declining rocks at her left and right were momentarily illuminated by the brilliant glare from the robots' lights. These rocky walls were falling vertically into the depth of the lake, and Ina advanced carefully deeper and deeper.
She didn't see a single living being on her way down. She just could hear the soft buzz of the diving robots. Then the machines stopped abruptly shining their lights into the dark. Deep underneath on the rocky ground Ina could see the vents towering towards her. Due to the steep walls it was almost impossible to avoid them. How for heaven's sake could she reach these damned fruits? And where could they actually be? She intensely scanned the illuminated rocky walls for plants. She went on swimming along the rift above the dangerous springs. Why didn't those robots follow her? What was the sense of these stupid machines anyway? Ina tried to remember Liess' words. Where did these healing plants grow? Apparently they grew in little niches in the rocks. But how could she find them without any light?
Ina let her hand slip into her bag looking for a lamp. She touched the gloves. Well, she would need them later.
She kept diving in the dark trying to stay always in the same depth to avoid the hot springs. Probably she was on the wrong side. But should she cross over to the other side? Simply penetrate into the pitch-black darkness? This was doomed to failure. She could return empty-handed or stay under water for the rest of her young life…
Disheartened she went back to the robots which had remained at the same place. She carefully observed the surroundings and decided to try her luck in the opposite direction. A faint glow far away attracted her attention. It was clearly visible, a feeble orange gleam midst the total darkness. Was it an animal? Or maybe a plant? Perhaps it was an Iao trying to help her to find the healing plants? Ina had a broad smile on her face when she approached the light. It was a small water plant packed with orange-

yellow fruits emerging from darkness. Obviously she was on the right way. Ina put on one of the gloves, carefully picked the first fruit, and harvested all the fruits from that plant. Afterwards she carefully closed her bag and continued the search. Then she saw another plant, but this one had a sort of shimmering blue pears, she also harvested. Further down she discovered more plants. Happily she dived from one healing plant to the next one. Ina didn't pay attention to the hot springs getting dangerously close to them while she was chasing behind more fruits. She had completely forgotten the urgent warnings about the rapidly increasing currents and their changing direction. The diving robots were far above her; she could barely see their lights.

Ina didn't have the slightest chance. A huge wave coming out of nowhere seized her and carried her many feet deeper down. Short after the first wave a second one reached her and pulled her even further down into the abysm. This repeated several more times; she was carried away like a leaf in the wind. Her left upper arm scraped painfully against a bizarre rock outcrop. Desperately she tried to swim against the current feeling the rocky hot water vents all around her until seconds later she reached the sandy lake bottom lying in a pitch-black night.

What should she do now? The pain in her arm got worse. And where was her bag? She must have lost it on her wild journey. At the moment this was the least important thing. She was on the bottom of this horrible rift without any connection to the outer world, injured and completely powerless by now.

She tried to detect the light from the robots, but it had disappeared. The water seemed to be warmer than before. Breathing had become much harder. She had to be careful and try to swim upward to reach cooler waters. But what was going on with that horrible current? Anyway, she had to get out of where she was now! But wait, wasn't there a circular light a couple of yards away from her? She could clearly see the fruit. They were all spread out on the floor emitting a diffuse light. She had to pick them up by all means. To move around cost Ina quite an effort. Her left upper arm hurt like hell, she had a pain in the gills when she was breathing, and she felt extremely weak. Finally she reached the place where the Gaia-fruit lay on the ground and she also saw the black shadow of her bag. Cautiously she began to pick up her harvest and put it into the bag. Again she was carried away by a wave, lifted up and hurled through the darkness. She tried to fight against it, but in vain. A few seconds later she lost her consciousness.

'We've got a technical problem', said one of the technicians. 'For any reason, the robots did not follow Ina. They positioned themselves on the upper end of the rift and just illuminated a small part of it.'
'What do you say? Does this mean that Ina is left in total darkness in the rift?' Farres asked. 'Well, the plants emit a weak phosphorescent light.'
'Yes, if Ina can find any', Farres said panting. 'She is away for too long.'
'That's not good at all', Ana reasoned. Her eyes wandered over the mirror-smooth lake surface. 'Where's the transporter platform?'
'It doesn't work either', explained Zaq, one of the technicians shrugging. 'It should have followed Ina on the surface, but we can't localize it anymore. At any moment it will return automatically to its loading station.'
'What a damned day is today!' Ana murmured, 'a thunderstorm is all that's missing.'
'Could we please search the lake?' Farres asked. His worries were written in his face.
'Folks', Ana said after a short call over the CC3. 'Ronok is also getting nervous. Shora has lost consciousness now and has not woken up for hours. She urgently needs medicine. I have requested reinforcement. Farres, the lake

will be searched in short.'
Farres nodded.
'Well, if Ina comes up to the surface, her microcomputer will send a signal, and we'll find her immediately', Okon concluded. He patted Farres encouragingly on his shoulder.

Ina had a strange dream. She was diving in the Loki Lake in complete darkness. A herd of Iaos carried her to the surface. They softly pushed the terrestrial woman with their snouts. Soft voices comforted her within her mind and gave her courage and power.

Ina took a deep breath, filled up her lungs, and opened her eyes staring into a pale blue sky. Her entire body was aching so much that she couldn't move. But she was alive, lying on her back drifting at the surface. It was good to breathe.
A dark shadow began to cover her. It was a glider. For a moment she rejoiced, but then she remembered the fruits she had harvested. She touched her shoulder looking for the shoulder strap of her bag. It was still there; she didn't lose it. She closed her eyes and fell unconscious.

'How can you say that', Farres said angrily. 'Ina risked her life for Shora; she almost died in the rift, and you dare to criticize her job.'
'She could have brought much more fruit, if she'd been more cautious. She has been advised and informed about the dangers several times. This shouldn't have happened', Ronok replied coldly.
'Ina was not the first one to be knowingly seized by the currents. It was accidental.'
'It was sheer stupidity, but I didn't expect any more from a terrestrial, but as you know, hope always dies last.'

'Compassion is completely unknown to you, isn't it?' Farres said furiously.
'Not necessarily', replied Ronok. 'Ina has failed miserably. I can't understand that. I admit that Shora may survive a few more months. But then what? In winter the lake is frozen and my daughter will probably die.'
Farres looked at Ina. She gently moved while she was sleeping.
'Look at her, Farres. She achieved to put herself out of action. If the Iaos hadn't saved her in the rift, she would have died down there. She has to take it easy for at least a week; the last summer days will pass by, and then another harvest will be impossible until early summer next year.'
Ina didn't look very well. Her left arm was badly bruised and completely grazed. Moreover, she had got many blue spots and her gill tissue was temporarily damaged.
Ina had listened to the two men for a while unnoticed. Now she couldn't conceal anymore that she was awake.
'How are you, darling?' Farres asked and sat down with his girlfriend taking her hand.
'I'm going to dive into the rift again. I can do it', she murmured.
'Don't be ridiculous, Ina', hissed Ronok. 'You had your chance. There won't be a second one', he said bitterly, 'at least not for Shora.'
'But…'
'Your harvest was too measly. Liess cannot make enough medicine from so few fruits. It can only secure her survival for a short time. You should have brought the blue pear-like water fruits.'
Ina clearly remembered Liess' words. These fruits had a tremendous healing power. They would have given Shora a new life, but somehow they had got lost. Ina bit on her lips.
'You lost them, didn't you?' Ronok asked threateningly. 'Do you know what I'd like to do with you?'

'Are you nuts?' Farres shouted and putting himself protectively in front of his girlfriend. 'Can't you understand that it wasn't intentional?'
'What's going on here?' Maris asked. She quickly wiped her cheeks; then she approached Ina.
Maris looked extremely sad. Ina was very concerned. She knew she had failed and… Her eyes were burning. 'I'm so sorry!' she said sobbing. In this very moment her pain didn't matter anymore and she didn't care what Ronok might do to her. She was predestinated to save the life of a young woman and mother, but she had failed. She could never be forgiven. Her own existence seemed small and unimportant to her.
'What did you do to her?' Maris asked her husband. She sat down next to Ina caressing her hair, but Ina avoided her touch and turned away.
'I didn't do anything yet. She lost the fruit which would have saved our daughter's life, do you understand?'
The old lady Liess had entered unnoticed the laboratory, shuffled to the group of people sitting together, and said: 'You know that it's not her fault, my love? She did her best.'
Ronok did not reply.
Ina was lying face down, her head hidden between her arms and wept uncontrollably. Her pain became unbearable; she was thirsty and couldn't support having failed.
'You have fever, child', Liess murmured with compassion while she was touching Ina's forehead. 'Just calm down! There's always a solution.'
Ina looked at her through tears and the old lady returned the look.
'Now you first have to get something against your pain and a good glass of water. Farres do us a favor and get something to drink.'
Farres nodded and did as he was told. The cool water Farres instilled her did her tremendously well. Liess had added a painkilling substance. That caused a wonderful,

relieving effect in less than two minutes. Ina closed her eyes and breathed much calmer.
'I don't like that fever at all', said Ronok thoughtfully. He turned to his computer.
'You don't really care for Ina as you can't benefit from her anymore', Farres scolded. 'So why should you care if she has fever or not?'
'Farres, she is hosting my experiment', Ronok replied angrily. 'That was and is the only reason why I spend my valuable time with that terrestrial woman!'
Maris sat in the seating corner in front of the large panorama window concealing her face between her hands. She felt weak, powerless, and tremendously desperate.
For a change, Liess shook her head because of Ronok's harsh words.
Farres turned to Ina who was staring silently into blank space. She had really hoped she could help to save Shora and obtain a place in this alien society. Now even Xio and Bora would reproach her for her mistakes, and perhaps even Sesa. Maybe she would have to live with her biological parents. She shuddered when she thought about it.
'Drink this!' Ronok requested holding a small flask with a tarry liquid under her nose.
'What is it?' Farres asked. He didn't trust the doctor anymore. Did he want to poison Ina with that stuff or was it the Yso-syrup?
'What do you think, Farres?' Ronok asked irritated. 'It's just a soporific mixed with an extract to reduce the fever. Don't worry; I'll care for your girlfriend until she's healthy again.'
'No, Ronok. You won't come close to her. Ana and Liess will do that.'
'Ina needs my help! You are risking her health. Do you want to do that?'
'But…'
'My dear Farres', Liess suddenly said in an unusually serious tone, 'Ronok still is the only one who can really

help Ina in an emergency case, and this is one. The fever has risen very fast and you know that your girlfriend is much more susceptible than other people due to the experiment.'

'Yes, that's true', Farres said angrily. 'And who takes the credit?'

'I don't do her any harm; you can trust me', Ronok sighed shaking his head.

Farres seemed irresolute. Everybody knew that Liess always told the truth outright and straightforward. She had no need to tell a lie.

'Please give Ina this medicine, Farres', Liess asked him. 'If it's coming from you, she'll accept it.'

Farres snatched the flask out of Ronok's hand and said annoyed: 'Ok, but only because I trust Liess!'

Ina slept for three entire days. When she finally woke up, Ana was sitting at her bed smiling at her with her sparkling blue eyes.

'Did you sleep well, my little princess?' she asked happily.

'Hallo Ana', Ina murmured and stretched contently. She was almost free of pain, but… 'Why am I in the laboratory?' she asked flabbergasted.

'You have been diving in the rift and got into a current', Ana explained.

'Oh no', Ina said sighing, 'Shora. I failed!' Her face turned pale.

'Forget it. Thanks to you Shora is doing well and at the moment this won't change. Ronok has overreacted. Meanwhile he has cooled down a bit. He was very disappointed as he thought his plan wouldn't work. Well, and Xio has summoned him to appear before the council of the delegates.'

Ina cast a questioning glance at Ana.

'Well, the experiment was very costly. As you know, it was funded through external sources and some of the sponsors want their money back. In their opinion the experiment did not pay off. This was treated in a public hearing.'

'What?'

'I don't really know, if I'm allowed to talk about this', Ana murmured insecurely.

Ina darted an angry look at Ana. 'They want Ronok to refund the costs', Ana said.

Ina got nervous. 'How can he do that? He has invested all his money in the diving robots.'

'They proposed he should present you as a show piece. People, who pay enough money, could watch you…' Ina screamed.

'Keep calm! Ronok rejected to do so. He just wanted to save his daughter and ensure her health care. He neither will sell nor exhibit you.'

'How can you be sure?'

'It has already begun', Ana replied. 'Do you know how many inquiries he has each day? Ronok is rejecting them all.'

'Ana, I have failed. Do you think he has adopted a different attitude by now? He was very furious about me because I couldn't help his daughter', Ina said gasping desperately.

'Ina', Ana shook her head, 'only yesterday he had a tremendous dispute with a former college friend of his because of you. Garos wanted to see you and learn more about you. He had traveled a long way to see you, but Ronok intercepted him and didn't let him into the lab. Is that clear enough?'

With an ice cold hand Ina brushed her reddish blonde curls out of her face. 'Ana, he hates me.'

'I don't want to talk about that', the Sathorjan replied. 'I've been working with Ronok for many years and I'm sure he won't hand you over. He is very aware of his duty and responsibility. The tiniest injury of your gill tissue might mean your death. Ronok knows that, Ina. I can't imagine that he wishes you suffering agonies.'

Ina sighed deeply and turned away. She had Shora on her conscience, and Ronok would let her feel sorry for her failure in whatsoever way. Even Maris was behaving in a different way now, and Ina wasn't sure if she was still enjoying her protection…

Ina bit into a large-leafed flower sucking and chewing on it without appetite. She poured so much water into her mouth that Ana was afraid she might drown.
Some minutes later without having pronounced a word Ina suddenly said pleadingly: 'Ana
you must help me!'
'Shall I call Farres?' Ana replied quickly looking at her CC3.
'No, I want to go back to dive in the rift once more.'
'What?'
'That's my only chance, don't you understand?'
'But that`s not possible, Ina! According to the weather report tomorrow is the last warm day. Afterwards a huge depression is approaching us, and we'll have thunderstorms, strong wind gusts, and hail.'
'Then I have to dive immediately!' Ina said with a firm voice. Ana was amazed.
'You are not yet completely recovered; your arm is badly bruised and…'
'Do my gills work properly?' Ina interrupted her.
Ana looked astonished at the terrestrial.
'Yes, I think so. The latest check hasn't shown any problems.' Ana paused for a moment, and then she said: 'You want me to help you to escape from the laboratory?'
When Ina nodded, Ana called out: 'Ina, you can't expect this from me. They'll fire me, if anything goes wrong!'
'Ana, I'll do it tonight!'
'How can you? You are completely mad!'
'During the night nobody will miss me. Alons will manipulate my CC3…' Ina covered her mouth with her hand observing Ana's reaction.

'Will he? Just forget it!' Ana said sighing deeply.
'Ana, please!'
'Can't you ask Farres?'
'He won't let me go', Ina concluded filled with bitterness.
'That's because the whole thing is crazy and dangerous. Why don't you ask Ronok? After all it's all because of his daughter.'
'Ask Ronok!' Ina croaked.
'Probably not a good idea', Ana sighed. 'He'll never let you dive in the lake in your actual state.'
Ina looked pleadingly at Ana. 'Please, help me!'
'I am crazy!' Ana said panting after a brief consideration. 'Ok, I'll help you. But first I have to talk to my friend. Maybe he can organize the diving robots and inform Alons. I wonder if your future brother-in-law will take part in your plan.' Ana stood up. 'If you don't need me anymore, I'll go and see what I can do.'
'Thank you, Ana.' Ina said with a broad smile on her face.
Two minutes later Liess came to see Ina.
'What makes you so confident?' she asked kindheartedly.
'Nothing', Ina lied.
'Really? You can tell an old woman the truth. Don't worry!'
Ina didn't tell, but she readily let her change the dressing and took obediently her medicine.
'The second time you'll do it', Liess said with a wink of an eye.
'How did you know?'
'I can see it in your face. You have new hopes. There's only one possible reason: You're going to dive in the rift again. Well, courage and perseverance doubtlessly are your best virtues.'
'Please…' Ina began, but Liess interrupted her.
'I won't tell anybody. It would cause you even more problems. Oh yes, before I forget it: The syrup you just took, will show an immediate effect. It will help against fatigue

and give you power.
'Thank you,' Ina replied.
'That's impossible!' Alons shouted into the lab. 'Hallo, Liess', he said a bit calmer.
Hallo, my dear', the herbalist greeted him.
'Do you know about Ina's crazy idea?' he asked furiously.
'Of course I do!'
'Ina, tell me: Are you crazy? You want me to help you to get out of the palace unseen?'
Ina nodded.
'What's wrong with you? That's not possible. I'll be risking my job, my existence!'
'You are constantly doing that', Liess replied quietly.
'But this is different. Ina is part of the family. It's extremely important, that it works out well. If Ina loses her life down there, I do not only lose my job, but also my family.'
'Don't worry, my dear. Our Ina will do it', Liess stated softly.
Alons looked pensively at Ina.
'Forget Shora and think a little of Farres', Alons said angrily. 'To me you don't look very fit, and it's irresponsible to dive into the rift in your state.'
'Alons, you don't understand. It's my destiny', Ina said looking sadly at the Sathorjan.
'Don't look at me this way', Alons looked away and said: 'You have been forced into this. It's not your destiny!'
'Ana said that Ronok will have to pay back the sponsors' money and…' She stopped.
'Oh yes? Actually Ana is talking too much', Alons commented angrily. 'And that's why you want to sacrifice your life? Didn't Ana tell you that Ronok doesn't want to sell you? He doesn't want somebody dissecting you, you understand?'
Ina shook her head.
'You don't trust him?' Alons said resigning.

'Well, it's like this', Liess explained. 'Her bold plan is it to earn her place the hard way.'
'You want Ronok's goodwill and respect, hmm? He is wearing you down with his psycho terror.'
Ina nodded and looked desperately at Alons.
'Okay! I'll switch off your CC3 tonight. Nobody will notice that you are diving in the lake. You have five hour. I can't get you any more time.'
Ina got up and hugged Alons. 'Thank you.'
'Don't overdo it. The period of time will be from 11 pm to 4 am. Please, keep to it.
Ina nodded.
'That's nice', Liess said when Alons had left. 'I'll return to my herbal kitchen to prepare everything. Be careful when you pluck the fruits. They are very delicate and may easily be damaged. Bring them directly to me. A ball robot will bring you the bag with the gloves. I'll tell Farres to let you alone today, so you aren't tempted to tell him about your plans. Ina cast a sullen look at Liess. 'That's better', murmured the old lady. She stroked over Ina's head, said good bye and left her alone.

Ina felt free and easygoing. She swam behind the diving robots and followed their lights ignoring the queasy feeling in her stomach.
The rocky cliff of the deep rift emerged in front of her. The robots had reached exactly the same position as the first time. Ina knew immediately, where she had to go. One of the machines started moving and followed her like a shadow along the rocky wall. At her side the rocky vents emerged from the sandy bottom. The strong currents had given them strange forms; they looked like bony fingers. Ina looked away.
But where were the water plants? Ina looked around searching then she suddenly stopped. She instinctively knew that she had to go deeper; otherwise she wouldn't find any fruits. Minutes later she discovered the largest and most beautiful plant she'd ever seen. Unfortunately it was growing at the foot of a high vent. How could she get there? She immediately recognized the plant with the luminous blue fruits. Cautiously she moved deeper and deeper. A wave seized her, but Ina clung firmly to a rock ledge and kept climbing downward. Don't let it go, she said to herself. Liess' medicine really had mobilized her strength, but it couldn't alleviate the pain in the arm. After climbing down for a while, she reached the bottom with her feet, but she hadn't taken in account the water temperature as high as 28 degrees down here and clearly too high for her. How long would she be able to resist until she lost her conscience?

Ina mustered all her courage and began to swim. She reached the plant quicker than she had expected. Delighted she grasped the first fruit, but then she recoiled. Oh no, she forgot to put on the gloves. Her right hand burnt like fire, as if she had put it into an anthill or touched a jelly fish. She quickly put on the wafer-thin gloves. Now the harvest could begin. When she stored away the last fruit, she felt a slight dizziness. It was imperative to reach immediately a cooler water layer. She pushed herself off the ground and was instantly carried away by a wave. This time she had closed very well the bag and started to fight against the current in total darkness. Ina wasn't able to distinguish upward from downward. An Iao emerged out of nowhere. It shone with its phosphorescent light.
'Follow me', it said in Ina's head.
The water calmed down a bit, as Ina followed the Iao. She wished she could see more of the creature than just the feeble glow.
'Here', the creature suddenly said.
'Oh, my God!' Ina thought and looked around. She was surrounded by a herd of Iaos. But that was nothing special. The water plants protruding from the rocks were indescribable. Full of fruit of all different kind they were shimmering in the dark water. Ina could hardly believe it.
'Take all you can carry. Afterwards we bring you to the machines.'
'Thank you. That's wonderful!' Ina replied in thoughts.
'Hurry up', the voice said in her head. Ina did as she was told. She filled up her bag and returned to the diving robots circulating unceasingly in the lake.
Ina came up to the water surface and climbed on the waiting transport platform which soon started moving. Gratefully she wrapped into the readily laid out, warm towel, took care of her gills with fresh Quados, and lay down on the small transporter. Satisfied with herself she gazed into the dark blue night sky. It was full of stars as

far as her eyes could reach; it was simply splendid. Yes, she was exhausted and had pain, but she had achieved to get enough fruits.
The palace was silent. The entrance hall was illuminated in the diffuse light of the night lighting. Ina was completely exhausted and closed her eyes.
'It's good that you are back!' Liess said suddenly. The transporter had stopped directly in front the old Sathorjan lady's herb kitchen.
Ina blinked when she saw the old lady. 'This time it worked', Ina said with a sigh and handed the bag over to Liess. The old lady looked into the bag and said with astonishment:
'That's incredible, Ina. The harvest is fantastic. You brought so many different fruits. Now I can make ineffably valuable medicines from these, not only for Shora. You have achieved an excellent result. I am proud of you!'
She extended her hand to help Ina to get down from the transporter and lie down on a comfortable bench.
'You should have a rest first, child.'
Ina nodded; then she murmured: 'Can you give me something against the pain?'
'Yes, of course', replied the Sathorjan. 'Sorry, I forgot. The best would be a soporific now.'
Ina drank a sweet juice, nestled on the sofa, and instantly fell asleep.
'How is it possible?' Ronok looked amazed at Liess. Maris and he had come to see Liess at half past tree in the morning. The news that Ina had been diving in the lake in the middle of the night harvesting a large amount of valuable water fruits caused tremendous astonishment.
'That's incredible', Maris stammered and rubbed her eyes. 'How has she been able to do this?'
'I would like to know as well', Ronok said.
'I have no idea', Liess replied. 'She is sleeping on the sofa over there.' Liess checked a glass tube against the light

examining the bubbling blue liquid inside the tube.
'Well, my dear friends, in a couple of minutes your daughter Shora is getting a medicine which should cure her in two weeks' time.'
Maris began to weep; she couldn't help it. All the tension from the last months was over now. Her husband took her into his arms and comforted her; the old lady silently smiled and dedicated to her work.
'Did Ina say anything before she fell asleep?' Ronok inquired. Thoughtfully he watched the sleeping young woman on the sofa.
'She just asked for a pain killer', replied Liess.
'That's no surprise to me. She touched one of the fruits without gloves.' Ronok had a closer look on one of Ina's hand in the weak light. 'That's typical for our terrestrial!' he murmured.
'Typical?' protested Liess. 'You should eventually reconsider your prejudices!'
'I'll bring her to the laboratory to have a closer look at her', Ronok concluded. 'Who knows, what else she has been doing down there.'
Maris shook her head and darted a meaningful look at Liess.
'She'll be all right', Liess commented.

'Shora, my dear', Maris murmured softly and stroked lovingly over her daughter's brittle hair. She was holding a small thimble-size jar filled with a dark blue viscous substance between her fingers.
Slowly Shora opened her eyes. She needed several minutes until she became completely awake.
'Mom, Dad? What?' She gasped heavily and continued her sentence tediously: 'Do-you-want…'
Shora knew that is was in the middle of the night. Outside there was a complete darkness without a sign of dusk.
'Tonight Ina has been diving in the rift again, and she has…' Maris burst into tears again.

Shora looked at her father without understanding. Ronok took the little jar from Maris and said: 'This is the first sip of the blue Mali-fruit extract. You know what that means!'
His daughter's eyes sparkled; her pale face began to smile in a moment of happiness.
Carefully Ronok dribbled the valuable substance onto his daughter's tongue.
'Now you'll get a little better every day', he explained softly.
Maris sat at Shora's side, held her hand, and shed tears of joy.

'Wake up, my darling', Farres began to talk softly in Ina's dream. Ina opened her eyes and looked at her friend with surprise.
'What are you doing in my bedroom?'
'Hey Ina, I love watching you when you are asleep. Then you're quiet and don't get secret adventurous ideas', Farres said smirking.
Ina punched him into his side. 'This was best for you; thus you didn't worry unnecessarily.'
'Unnecessary? Ronok told me a different story!'
'Did he?'
'You have been gadding around in the hot ground layer again and you touched at least one fruit without the gloves! You have been climbing on the rocky walls, got into the current, and you have been brought back by your friends, the Iaos, to save you from the worst.'
Ina looked at Farres with amazement. 'How do you know that?' Had she talked while she was sleeping? Or had Liess told him about her excursion?
'As you can imagine, Ronok examined you thoroughly. Well, your body reveals it all.'
'Just stop it!' Ina scolded him. She softly stroked over the bandage prepared with plants around her right hand.
'You have been sleeping for five days and nights, until Ronok agreed to let you out of the lab.'
'Well, you can take it as a sort of reward not to wake up surrounded by machines once more.' Farres smirked again. 'It's much more comfortable here.'

Ina sank back into her bed. Farres lay down in the bed next to her and kissed her. 'You did it, darling. Shora is getting better. She would like to see you to thank you.'
'What? Today?'
'Today!' Farres said sighing and tried to kiss her again. However, she turned away and sat up.
'What's the problem', he asked. 'The whole story with Shora is unpleasant for me.'
'Just don't think about it, darling. Enjoy your success and…' He caressed her cheek tenderly.
'I will', Ina replied happily. She snuggled with her friend and enjoyed his hugs and kisses. Yes, she truly loved Farres. She just had to ask that question even though she would destroy that romantic moment: 'Could you imagine having kids with me?'
'Pardon me?' Farres asked startled and sat up. 'How did you get that idea?'
'I don't know', Ina replied insecurely.
'Let's see! As far as I know we belong to the same species', Farres deduced smirking. 'Anyway, in your special case you'll probably have to consult Ronok for permission.'
'That's not funny', Ina noted annoyed. 'You did not answer my question.'
'Yes darling, I could imagine very well. But it's still a bit too early. We don't know each other for a long time yet. I don't know how you handle this on Earth, but on Sathorja the family planning takes a little longer.'
'It was just a basic question', Ina murmured embarrassed. 'I don't really know why I asked.'
'I do!' Farres replied grinning and began to undress Ina.

Less than an hour later Ina went to see Shora. Farres allegedly had to go to a meeting with his boss. Ina didn't believe a word. For some reason he didn't want to come with her, although she badly needed his help.
Ina crossed though the center of the palace – the hall of mirrors. She loved that room; each time it was worth the

detour. Unconfidently she looked at herself in the mirror. She was looking very pretty with her long reddish blonde hair and the emerald green dress. She straightened up, looked into her eyes again, and strolled on. When was she supposed to be with Shora? In ten minutes. She had to hurry up.
Out of breath she was standing in the door opening of Shora's room. Everybody was there: Ronok and Maris with all their children, children-in-law and grandchildren were sitting happily around Shora's bed. The old lady Liess was also there having an animated discussion with a dark haired woman, Ina didn't know. The three kids, the eldest not older than six, were running around the room.
'There's Ina!' shouted a five year old girl.
Instantly everybody in the room looked at Ina and applauded. Ina immediately blushed. Actually she had hoped to meet Shora alone.
'Please, come in', the young woman asked her with a clear voice. When Ina looked at Shora, she didn't believe her eyes. Was it really Maris and Ronok's sick daughter? Her hair, before white and brittle, was now of gold blonde color, she had rosy cheeks, and her skin had lost its pale complexion.
She seemed to be full of life. What a tremendous effect these fruits had. This was incredible!
'Ina, it's you! Don't look at me so puzzled!'
'You are late', said Ronok reproachfully.
'That doesn't matter, Dad', opined Piru, Ronok's son. Ina remembered him well as she had met him recently in water world.
'Well, may I present you to my family: Kun, my husband, and Voni and Tria, my daughters. The girls smiled at Ina, but Kun looked a bit reserved.
'Nimi, my little sister and her husband Vons and Gob, their son. You already know my dear brother Piru.' She paused and then she said: 'Thank you very much!'

'Don't mention it', Ina replied shyly.
'How are you, Ina?' Nimi asked. She didn't look like her elder sister at all. She had short, dark, and curly hair and a roguish, but open and friendly face.
'I'm well', Ina murmured. She turned to the door and wanted to leave.
'Wait. You have seen the Iaos, didn't you?' Voni asked with sparkling eyes.
'Yes, I did', replied Ina.
'Are they really so colorful shining with their own light?' Gob asked curiously.
'Indeed', answered Ina. 'They are very beautiful.'
'Please, tell us all about them!' cried the two girls. They took Ina's hand, led her to an arm chair and climbed cheerfully on her lap. Gob also sat in front of her on the floor. Ina couldn't help but tell the kids about the strange water creatures in all detail. The kid's presence calmed down the terrestrial. She loved to talk to them and told them everything about her adventures under water. She also mentioned the place the Iaos had shown to her, where she had found most of the fruits.
'Is it true, Ina?' Piru asked with astonishment. 'You have been together with these Iaos? Do you know where they live?'
'I have been following them. They wanted me to do so.'
'Wow Ina', Nimi called out enthusiastically. 'That's incredible! Nobody has ever been in contact with these shy creatures, just you!'
It became silent. Shora's daughters had come back to her mother's bed and cuddled against her. The small ones hadn't had their mother for a long time. But now Shora hugged and kissed the girls. Then she looked at Ina and said seriously: 'I hope you didn't suffer much because of me. I am really sorry you had to endure so many hardships. I don't know how to make up for the damage. The only thing I can offer you is my friendship.' She extended her hand; Ina got up and shook it. Nimi, Shora's younger

sister, unexpectedly embraced Ina. 'Thank you for saving my sister. Without her the entire family would have broken up.'
'Ina', said Piru, 'I have to admit that you have really done a good job. I never would have thought you could do this and I think I also speak for my father.' Piru cast a meaningful look at Ronok.
'Thank you, Ina', Maris said panting and embraced her all of a sudden.
'I think, I also owe you a thank you', Ronok said after a long pause. 'I have estimated you entirely wrong.' Ina stared at him with a mixture of fear and astonishment. 'Ina, I have to apologize.' These words encouraged her to shake her archenemy's hand; in a way making peace with him. Again the room was full of resounding applause. Maris hugged her husband. Liess blinked an eye at Ina who was trying to leave the room.
'And what is going on with the sponsors of the experiment?' Kun, Shora's husband asked.
Ina stiffened and turned around.
'The matter is closed', explained Ronok. 'Ina has been a great success, and all the criteria have been met. The money was not spent in vain, so the majority of the sponsors are satisfied.'
'You are missing the chance of a lucrative business', objected Kun.
'What do you mean?' Ronok wondered.
'Your experiment might have made you rich and famous, don't you understand? Ina is your property; you are not accountable to anybody.'
Was Shora really married to that guy? He was disgusting.
'Kun, what are you babbling?' Shora asked indignantly. Her eyes wandered to Ina who was looking at Kun with dismay.
'Kun, let me explain', Ronok said particularly quiet. 'Ina is not a movable asset, but a human being.'

'How can you say that?' Kun said disdainfully. 'You have taken great advantage of the fact that she is just a terrestrial.'
'I'm afraid you're right', said Ronok. 'But since she risked her life for Shora, I changed my opinion about her, and you should do so, too.'
'Why? Remember what her parents did to you', Kun shouted angrily.
'Yes, but Ina has already suffered enough from the fact that she is Chris and Elsa's daughter', Ronok concluded shortly. 'I had the intention to torment them doing the experiment with their daughter and to teach them a lesson. I always kept them up to date, and they had no way to help her. I wanted to make them suffer the same I suffered those days in the space ship. I had no way to control the virus they introduced from Earth. Three Sathorjans died, and some of them still are suffering the consequences of that insidious disease today.'
'You never told me!' Shora murmured affected. 'I thought you just wanted to save me.'
'Yes, of course. That was the primary reason. But even today I still hate Elsa and Chris. In those days I almost lost my license to practice medicine, and they could have put me in prison.'
'You never mentioned that', said Shora. 'Why should they put you in prison? It wasn't your fault.'
'In a certain way it was. I failed to immunize all the passengers against the strain of virus from Earth.'
Ina was getting dizzy. Why was Ronok telling that story?
'But there are enough reasons to present Ina to the scientists. Why do you take compassion on her? I don't understand you.'
'Kun, actually it's not Ina's fault. How would you feel, if you were punished for something your parents did?'
'Do you mean a sort of kin liability?' asked Vons.
'It's obvious that we've done Ina deeply wrong', Ronok said sternly. 'Ina is equivalent to us, and I'm not going to

sell nor exhibit her. I don't mind money or fame.'
Kun stood up and left the family meeting without saying a word. Shora shook her head fretfully while she was hugging her daughters tenderly. She felt it was time to separate from her husband. They had nothing in common anymore except for their daughters.
Nimi looked at Liess. The old woman turned to Ina.
'Are you all right?' she asked her.
'Yes', Ina said a little confused.
'I congratulate you', said Liess. 'Now you have reached your objective.'
She smiled at Ina, and Ina returned the gesture.
'Ina', Ronok said, 'if you want to leave, you can go now.'
Ina nodded gratefully, said good bye, and left the room.

The days went by and fall arrived accompanied by its freak weather conditions. Shora returned to her usual life. Kun preferred to go back to his home town. He seldom came to visit his little daughters.
From time to time Ina met Shora. She liked to talk to the young woman and see how happy she was with her children. She met Nimi, Shora's younger sister every second day in water world. Her son Gob participated in a diving course for kids Ina supervised together with a diving teacher. Yes, Ina had been assigned a job, and that was good. She felt accepted and useful. Looking after the kids in the water was quite exhausting. Sometimes she had to pull somebody out of the lake. Nevertheless she enjoyed it.
The meetings with Sesa were not so amusing. Her sister had finished school, passed all the exams, and was free now. Unfortunately she was often bored, so Ina had to sacrifice and spend the afternoons with her.
Farres had gone on a long business trip. It had to do with security systems. Ina didn't know much about it, but she missed him.
'Hallo Sesa!' Ina said when they met at the exit of water world. 'I'd like to have a rest one day. I'm very tired. The kids have been exhausting. I don't want to comb through the boutiques now.'
'But Ina, I want to show you some novelties. I got something new for you.' Sesa looked at her pleadingly.
Sesa persuaded her and her sister accompanied her to one of the wonderful patios at the palace.

'That's dream-like', Ina said appreciatively when they passed through the high glass door entering the patio. The garden was dominated by narrow, highly grown trees reaching up to the fifth floor. Rain was falling noisily on the glass roof spanning the inner court yard. Arcades with uncountable seats on different levels made the patio quite comfortable. Ina could see a pond in the center. It was shimmering in an emerald green color inviting for a swim.
Although she would have liked to refresh herself in the water, Ina sat down with Sesa on a bench under a cobalt blue coniferous tree.
'What are you thinking of?' Sesa asked curiously. She picked a flower from a bush next to her and put it into her mouth.
'Oh', Ina said panting, 'I miss Farres. Since many days he's away now, and I have no news from him. I don't understand why he had to go anyway. His brother should have gone instead.'
'Ina, they need Alons at the palace. Next week there'll celebrate the great festival. The preparations are in full swing. We have never sent so many invitations, and you can imagine that the security measures will be tremendous.
'What are they celebrating?' Ina asked surprised.
'They celebrate peace in the solar system', Sesa explained.
'Do they?'
'As there are lots of different people on different planets and moons, peaceful agreement is not a matter of course. Therefore we celebrate the festival of solidarity at this time every year.'
Ina looked at her with amazement.
'This will be very interesting for you, Ina', Sesa commented. 'There are lots of different life forms: Earth creatures, air borne beings, water creatures…'
'Mixed-up creatures like me!' Ina grunted.
'Oh no, I think you are unique', Sesa said thoughtfully.

'I don't know if I want to go to that festival', Ina's eyes were wandering from one window to the next.
'Ina, you mustn't let this opportunity slip.'
'I will, Sesa. I don't like aliens. I'm scared of them.'
'Dangerous creatures are not allowed to enter the palace.'
'And if somebody wants to learn about the experiment?'
'You just get rid of him.'
'I just don't feel very well about it', Ina murmured.
'Come on, my dear, it's a wonderful opportunity to participate in a Sathorjan festival! Please! It won't be fun without you!'
'As I probably stay here for the rest of my life, I'll have lots of opportunities to attend festivals like this.'
'Farres' family is coming and you'll meet my aunts and cousins. They're offering a huge show and you'll see the biggest and most beautiful hall for the first time.'
'I thought I already knew it.'
'No, it's only used for really great events. It's situated in the fourth basement floor and it's as large as the entire palace.'
'There are subterranean gardens with springs, secluded places…' Sesa paused.
'What's up?'
'During the festival last year I met a very sweet guy. Well, we retreated into a niche and…'
'I don't want to know', Ina cried and lifted up her hand protectively.
'We just kissed each other; what do you think?' Sesa replied offended.
'It's okay', Ina said conciliatorily. She stood up wandering around fascinated between wonderfully flowering plants and let her fingertips stroke over sap green leaves. She went to the pond, sat down on its edge, and stuck her hand into the water.
'Ina, what are you doing?'
'Nothing', she said looking up to her sister.
'I suppose you know that it's not a swimming pond?'

'Well, my CC3 says something else', Ina replied.
'You're nutty as a fruit cake. You've just been in the water. Can't you resist just once?'
'The water is wonderful.' She had taken off her shoes and put her feet into the pond.
Sesa shook her head angrily. 'Tell me if you're coming to the festival.'
'I don't know yet', Ina replied. She saw a slim silhouette approaching them from behind her sister.
'Shouldn't you always be in the water, you fishy woman?' Rida asked sweetly. She joined the two young women and looked at them disdainfully as if she found them disgusting.
'Rida, get lost!' Sesa nagged. 'We have to talk privately.'
'Oh, that's delightful!' Rida said purring. 'I have too!'
She turned to Ina. 'You are hailed as a heroine. For sure it's a fantastic feeling having saved one of us, isn't it?'
Ina didn't understand Rida's intention.
'You know', the blonde Sathorjan continued, 'you probably think you've paid your debt, and all the nice people who paid for the experiment are content. Well that's not the case; by no means! People say you should be made available to science. Oh, there are lots of potential buyers who would like to investigate you. It's a stroke of luck for an inferior creature like you!'
'Where did you get this nonsense from?' Sesa asked furiously.
'Oh, that's a fact', replied Rida firmly and turned to Ina again. 'Well, if you don't do it voluntarily, you will be obliged. Your beloved Farres will lose interest soon, when you are passing your miserable existence only in front of the media spotlights.'
Ina didn't know what to say when Rida walked away from her like a beautiful swan from an ugly duckling.
Sesa tried to defuse Rida's gossip, but Ina didn't want to listen to her. She left the patio in a hurry and run through the palace back to her flat. There she threw herself on the sofa and wept without restraint.

'Darling, what's wrong? We didn't see each other for a week, and you are behaving so strangely. Are you angry with me?' Farres asked his girlfriend startled.
'No', she replied scantly avoiding his look.
'Aren't you pleased? Today is a very special day. The festival of solidarity is a wonderful thing.'
'Yes, I know', she said. She sat down on the sofa and concealed her face in her hands.
'Ina! I don't understand', Farres said sighing. He sat down beside his girlfriend and looked at her thoughtfully. 'Are you afraid of something?'
'You better ask Sesa', Ina said panting.
'Wouldn't you like to tell me yourself?' Farres asked impatiently.
Ina stood up and went to the panorama window. She pushed her forehead against the cool glass and remained motionless for seconds. Then she felt Farres hands on her shoulders. 'Please, let me know!' asked the Sathorjan his girl from Earth.
Ina turned to him and told him slowly about her involuntary meeting with Rida.
'What?' Farres asked surprised. 'That's complete nonsense!'
'I don't want to go to this festival, Farres! Maybe she's waiting for me and…' Ina stopped and wiped the tears from her cheeks.
'Darling, please trust me!' Farres beautiful dark eyes looked pleadingly at Ina. 'Nobody will bother you because of your gills. You'll be protected, believe me.'

'Protected by you?'
'Not only by me, darling. During such a great event there are tremendous security measures. Furthermore, you are Sesa's sister, so you'll be more cared for than any other visitor.'
Ina didn't say anything.
'Please come with me to the festival. I'll be very happy to spend a wonderful evening with you. I have been missing you so much; every day without you is a lost day.'
'Yeah, you had lots!' Ina argued.
Farres hugged his girlfriend and kissed her tenderly.
'Do you think we have some time left before the festival?' Farres asked innocently.
'Hmm, perhaps a couple of minutes', Ina replied smiling, took his hand, and pulled him upstairs into the bedroom.

Less than an hour later, Ina and Farres were in the entrance area of the events hall. Huge glass sculptures pointed to the entrance gate. Robots, aliens, and men equally battled their way through that bottleneck.
For this evening Ina had prepared her hair and dressed up in Sathorjan style. She didn't want to attract too much attention at any price or create a negative impression. She had pinned up her reddish blonde hair and put some iridescent jewelry into it. The dress was shimmering in blue color shades changing its color with the incoming light. It was short and waisted. Farres liked it… Ina tried not to show her nervousness, when she strode apparently self-assured through the mighty hall with her boyfriend. Tables and chairs were floating in niches; plants decorated the walls which this time were not transparent. The floor was covered with colorful tiles, and every step triggered a light pulse. A subdued lighting made up for a cozy atmosphere in the hall. Trees grew up to the ceiling which Ina couldn't even see. This room had to be extremely high!

'Come with me, darling', Farres said pulling her between two flower pots. 'I know a shortcut.'
There were tables everywhere as far as the eye could reach. All of them were serviced, equipped with chairs, and illuminated by a strange light. In the center of this symmetrical circular arrangement Ina saw a large stage.
'What is this platform for?' Ina asked intrigued.
'Well, speeches will be held, among others by Xio and the chairman of the delegates' council of the United Planets'
Ina followed Farres to a table where Mula and Zed were sitting. Ina was overjoyed.
'Nice to see you, Ina', said Mula and hugged the terrestrial girl. Zed shook her hand and asked: 'How are you? Is everything okay again?'
'You have achieved great things, my love!' Mula said when Ina sat down beside her.
'That was a matter of course', Ina replied with reddened cheeks.
'You must not be so modest!'
Ina looked around. The tables were slowly filling up. A low murmuring could be heard. Although Ina couldn't see the entire hall, to her it looked even larger than the departure lounge of an airport on Earth.
She didn't see anybody she knew and had no idea where Sesa was. She hadn't seen her since the incident with Rida. Xio and Bora opened their way up through the crowd.
'In a few minutes the opening ceremony will take place', Zed explained.
'Hallo, my dear friends', Ina heard a soft female voice beside her. 'Are you all right?'
'Hallo, Tunia!' Mula said pleased. 'Yes, we are all right.'
'I have to care for some more people over there.'
'Don't let us keep you.'
Ina's eyes followed the woman und stuttered: 'Wasn't that a TFR?'
'Oh yes, she looks exactly like a woman, doesn't she?'

'Indeed', Ina said panting. She couldn't look away from the robot.
'Admit that you're afraid,' said Alons.
'No, I'm not', Ina said briefly.
'Alons, sit down with us', his mother prompted. 'Where did your sister go?'
'She's over there talking to a Zwoni. In fact Kara was talking to a frizzy-haired creature less than six feet tall. Its violet eyes were sparkling excitedly.
'Are you sure, she doesn't need help?' Mula asked worried. 'They say the Zwonis are not exactly peaceful creatures.'
'She's our daughter; she'll make it', commented Zed reassuring.

Xio held the opening speech. Lengthily he talked about the necessary economic and political community. Each planet and each people had to be mentioned and greeted expressively. As if his speech hadn't been long enough, after him an elderly lady rose to the podium.
Ina didn't listen to the speeches. She leaned against Farres' shoulder looking into the air and waiting ardently for the dinner. So far the festival had not impressed her exceedingly. She had to admit, the hall was imposing, although she had only seen a small part of it. Where were the wells, ponds and hidden forests? Oh yes, the water. It simply would be nice to submerge.
She had been diving at water world for many hours, but her body wished to do so again.
Ina had almost fallen asleep when squadrons of ball robots eventually turned up serving a great variety of food. The lighting and the atmosphere had made her extremely tired.
'Darling, are you asleep?' Farres asked in a low voice striking softly over her hair.
'Excuse me', Ina said sighing and straightening up immediately. Kara and Alons smirked at her.

'It's not very exciting, isn't it?' said Kara. Ina shook her head.
'I don't like these events very much', Kara explained while scooping a blue flower dish on her plate. 'It usually takes a long time until the party picks up steam, but then it is fun.'
Ina nodded and concentrated on the delicious food. Wow! Liess and her team of robots had exceeded her expectations. Ina began to feel comfortable. She enjoyed being together with Farres' family so she didn't want to accompany Farres, when he asked her to do so.
'Come on Ina! There's much more to see than just the dining room.'
'But I'm too tired', Ina said gasping, when he took her by the hand.
'Then it's high time to walk around to cheer up', remarked Farres.
Together they strolled to a small lake in the middle of a little park. Many guests had gathered there, sitting on benches, talking, laughing, and drinking a pink liquid from narrow, high glasses.
'She did it again', Ina said gasping and pointed to her CC3.
Farres read Rida's message shaking his head. 'Just forget it, darling!'
'But she wrote something terrible is going to happen!'
'That's nonsense!'
Ina didn't want to spoil the evening with her fear, so she ignored Rida's message. They crossed over a narrow footbridge spanning over a lake.
'This is simply precious!' Ina said when they stopped on the bridge.
'Now we are exactly in the center of the events hall', he explained. 'In front of us there are several rooms on various floors dedicated to the different planets. Are you interested or should we better look for a more secluded place?'

'Indeed you are insatiable.' Ina smiled and kissed him on the cheek. 'Maybe later. I'm interested in the place, where my parents have to live.

'Glosua? Well, if you wish', Farres said disenchanted. 'But you won't see much there.'

Ina had to use an almost invisible elevator again, but this time she bravely kept her eyes open. A little dizzy she left the lift on the seventh floor.

She seemed to be in another world, when they passed through an oval door. The air temperature was lower, and they were surrounded by a barren landscape. She just saw gnarled bushes while walking over short brown grass. An unpleasant wind was blowing into her face. The two suns illuminating the gloomy scene seemed to be further away.

'Ina!' a familiar voice was unexpectedly calling through the room. Ina turned around looking in all directions, but she couldn't see anybody.

'Farres?'

'What's wrong, darling?'

'Please, could we leave?' Ina anxiously looked at Farres. She had the hunch she might go mad. She just had heard her mother's voice.

'Ina!'

'No!' Ina screamed and closed her ears.

'Is anybody there?' Farres asked into the silence.

'It's me, Elsa!'

Farres stopped abruptly, when he saw a slender silhouette appearing from the darkness. Ina's eyes widened.

'How did you get here, Elsa?' Farres asked surprised. He just knew that woman from hearsay. He had never personally met Ina's parents. But he had heard many stories about them.

'Chris and I were invited to come here', she explained.

'But that's impossible! Xio and Bora would never endorse it.' Farres said as if he was talking to himself.

'I don't know who it was.' Elsa murmured.

'Where's your husband?' Farres asked looking around.
'He couldn't endure in here. He mixed up with the guests.'
Ina stared horrified at that woman. She could hardly remember her mother, but now she did, being face to face to her after fifteen years of loneliness.
'Why did you let me down?' Ina stammered deeply shocked.
'We could do nothing else, my dear. We feared for our lives. Your father had financially overstretched with a project; we were ruined and owed a lot of money to a shady organization. They threatened us. They would have taken Sesa away from us and sold her, if we couldn't pay back all the money.'
Elsa slowly approached Ina, but Ina backed off.
'Let me embrace you, child', she murmured.
'No!' Ina shook her head and looked into her mother's face for the first time. She seemed to be extremely tired and marked by the last years. She looked considerably older, her hair was white, and her body was emaciated.
'Please Ina, forgive me!' Elsa moaned. 'It was terrible for me to have to abandon you, believe me!'
'I was absolutely certain that my entire family had died', Ina screamed at her exasperated. 'Do you know how my childhood has been? Being an orphan? How could you do that to me?'

Meanwhile Farres had informed his brother. Alons belonged to the few people who had been in contact with Ina's parents. A couple of years ago he had assumed Zaq's job and was responsible for the supervision of the two. If there were any problems, he was the one who had to be notified.
A few minutes later Alons rushed into the room enraged and shouted at Elsa: 'Who has smuggled you in? I asked you and Chris to keep quiet and serve your sentence!'
'Hallo Alons', Elsa said with a sigh, 'please don't shout at

me. I wished to leave Glosua, and the chance was tempting: We had an invitation to the palace and we could see our children one more time.'
'Who was it?' Alons asked visibly nervous.
'Day before yesterday a nice man came to our home and told us that Chris and I were allowed to enter Sathorja. I don't know his name.'
'What was he like?'
'I can't tell. I couldn't see his face even though he stood directly in front of me.'
'A face distorter', Alons said shaking his head. 'Where is Chris?'
'He's looking for Sesa.'
'Oh no! If you two are discovered, there will be a tremendous hubbub, and I'll get problems. You have to get away from here without attracting attention.'
'But…'Elsa looked at him desolately.
'If Bora knows you're here, she'll get a nervous breakdown. And Ronok? What do you think is he going to do?' Alons asked bitterly.
'That crazy doctor', Elsa said disdainfully. 'I'd never thought that he would go as far as to torture our daughter.' Her eyes wandered to Ina.
'This is not possible. You have to get out of Sathorja', Alons said sighing. 'Farres, you stay with Elsa and Ina. I'll try to find Chris.'
Suddenly a glaring light filled the room. Ina couldn't open her eyes for a while, but she heard Xio's loud voice: 'That's a scandal. How is it possible, Alons?'
'I didn't know anything about it', the young man explained himself. When Ina had got used to the light, she noticed the turmoil her parents had caused.
Sesa stood weeping beside her adoptive mother who had turned deadly pale observing the unreal scene with empty eyes. Elsa and Chris stood in front of Ina, but there were surrounded by a cage made up with blue laser rays. Farres had laid his hands on Ina's shoulders, as if

he wanted to stop her from running to her parents. But actually she had no such plans.
'This can't be true!' Losos, the chief of the security department, said.
'I really have nothing to do with it.' Alons was getting hot.
'Then who did it?' Losos asked furiously. He called his office and began to yell desperately trying to find out, who had been the last one being in contact with Ina's parents.
Bora suddenly fainted and fell backwards. Luckily she was intercepted by her robot that could prevent her falling down. Xio ran to his wife and shouted: 'Bring Ronok here immediately!'
Sesa didn't budge. It looked as if she didn't even notice Bora. She stared at her biological parents as if she was spellbound. Ina would have loved to know what was going on in her head.
'Let us be with our daughters!' Elsa begged in tears. 'We are a family. You can't take them away from us.'
Sesa made a tremendous leap forward – the laser cage evaporated into thin air – and she flung her arms around her mother's neck.
'Mom', she sighed.
Ina couldn't understand her sister. To Sesa, Elsa was an entirely strange woman except from the biological relationship. Both women had almost nothing in common.
'Ina, come here!' Elsa called out.
'You belong to us', remarked Chris and waved her to him. But Ina shook her head and stayed with Farres.
Meanwhile Ronok had arrived accompanied by his wife Maris. He deliberately ignored the terrestrials and cared for the unconscious Bora.
'Sesa, come here at once! Your mother is not well. She needs you.'
'She's not my mother!' replied Sesa bitterly.

'Are you out of your mind?' Xio asked appalled. He stood up incredulously staring at Sesa.
'I want to live with my parents.'
'But…'
'As you see', Chris said, 'the blood ties are stronger.'
'What can you offer her?' Xio asked him.
'Admittedly we have not much of material value to offer, but we can give them love and caring.'
'Xio, let us live here and…' begged Elsa.
'What are you asking for?' Ronok turned to the terrestrial. 'You're going to ruin us all!'
'Don't be ridiculous!' Ina's father shouted with a booming voice. 'What can we do?' He took a deep breath and said: 'You have destroyed our family without any justification, Ronok. We were innocent, just anxious people from Earth hiding in the space ship as our only retreat.'
'You should never have entered that space ship', Ronok replied. 'Three Sathorjans have died due to your virus. I had no chance to save them. Do you know how long they have accused me because of that? I was summoned before the delegate's council and almost lost my job.'
'And we had to vegetate on that ugly planet for decades devoid any contact with our daughter Sesa', Elsa remarked with a husky voice. 'As if that weren't bad enough, you turned our Ina into an amphibian. She can never lead a normal life again and will always be disfigured.'
'I don't have to comment this', Ronok said coldly.
'You have had your revenge!' Chris shouted angrily. Then he turned to Ina: 'I hope you know where you belong to. You don't have to stay with these crazy people. You should live with us.'
'We could be a family again', Elsa insisted and cast an almost imploring look at Ina.
'No', Ina replied firmly. 'You abandoned me in those days. Now it's too late. I don't need my parents anymore; I can get along very well without you.'

'Ina, we couldn't do otherwise', Chris grumbled. 'Don't be silly. Don't forget your roots. We are your parents. I don't know what you are expecting from these narcissistic and arrogant Sathorjans. They did the worst to you; nevertheless you turn away from us.'

Ina didn't say a word. All this was too much for her. She just longed for 'water world' and wished to be lonesome and quiet.

'That's enough', Xio said after a minute of silence. 'Sesa, you are coming back with us at once. Otherwise I'll tell the robot to bring you to your room.'

Bora sighed faintly. She was fully conscious again. Supported by Maris she stood up and looked desperately at her daughter.

'No', Sesa screamed hysterically, ran away from them, and disappeared though the door opening. Ina followed her.

'Sesa!' she called her. But Sesa kept on running and didn't even turn around. Shortly afterwards Ina had lost sight of her. Ina stopped gasping in the middle of the huge hall and looked around. Strange aliens went by chatting animatedly. She returned to the little lake and walked onto the footbridge. But she couldn't see the exit. Where might it be? Presumably Sesa had left the festival. She no longer had a reason to stay. But Ina didn't want to disappear just like this. Well, the encounter with her parents had stirred up her blood, but she didn't want to leave her boyfriend alone who had been looking forward to spend this evening with her. Ina decided to return to Farres when she saw a strange message from Sesa on the CC3. What? Sesa wanted to meet her sister on a toilet outside the events hall? Astonished she followed the instructions of her CC3. Well, they had to talk. Particularly she wanted to tell Sesa not to treat her adoptive parents that badly.

'Are you leaving already, my dear?' Liess asked Ina abruptly.

'Sesa has problems', Ina replied. She was glad to meet the old lady. 'She wants to talk to me.' Ina told Liess the whole story.
'This is very strange', the herbalist said thoughtfully. 'You have to be careful; the security system might be faulty. Usually is not so easy to smuggle in prisoners like your parents. It's quite odd that Alons didn't know about it.'
Ina's CC3 was peeping again.
'I must go', Ina said looking at her bracelet.
'It's all right, my dear. I'll tell Farres when I see him.'
'Thank you!'
It was strange. The corridor in front of the entrance area of the events hall was completely deserted. Not even a robot crossed her way. Ina went to the rest rooms. But there was no sign of Sesa. Where had her sister gone?
All of a sudden several giant figures appeared directly in front of her. She heard Sesa crying: 'No!' Seconds later Ina fell to the ground unconsciously...

Meanwhile the tension between the Sathorjans and the terrestrial couple had abated. After a couple of punches Elsa and Chris had been taken in custody. However they were allowed to stay at the palace for an indefinite period of time.
After the incident Xio tried to keep his guests entertained. A music ensemble was playing some cheerful, although a little odd melodies on a stage from light and glass. Bora had sat down at the table with her siblings telling them in tears about the terrible scandal.
Losos went to the security department together with Alons and Nuna. Farres went back to his parents who were chatting with old friends about the good old times. He thought Ina would come back soon.
Ronok and Maris disappeared among the many guests enjoying the great variety of entertainment facilities...

When Ina woke up, she was floating in the water feeling strong nauseas. When she opened her eyes and looked around, she saw that she was in a crystalline water tank the size of a coffin. Panic-stricken she touched the surrounding walls. She could turn round, but was unable to stand up. There was not enough freedom of movement. She felt like paralyzed by ineffable fear and vertigo.

As if that weren't bad enough, she was not alone. They were watching her! A tall, extremely lean figure stood in front of her prison staring penetratingly at her. Beside him was a woman with red eyes. They were talking; Ina couldn't hear anything, but she could see them. One of the aliens peeped into her tank that was floating in a room with grey, metal walls. Damn, where was she?

Only now she saw Sesa. She sat weeping in one corner of the inhospitable, artificially illuminated chamber. Ina could see her clearly; her shoulders moved with each sob. She had concealed her face in her hands; her wrists were bound.

Oh, she felt dizzy. She had to close her eyes, her stomach turned around, and her surroundings were dangerously wavering. She was not a fish in an aquarium; she had to get out of this tank. But just a moment! They had been kidnapped! Rida's words echoed in her head. Oh, no! Rida had arranged their abduction. She had mentioned it several times. Now she had managed to get rid of them. What was happening to them now? With all her force she knocked against the glass panes. She tried to lift up the

cover of her glass coffin with her legs just a little bit. Due to the effort she fainted again. The terrestrial girl was drifting unconsciously in the tank.
'Get Ina out of that tank', the lean man ordered a robot. 'Are you able to find out, what's wrong with her?'
'The water disables my sensors', the machine said with a rasping voice.
'Zaq,' Garos shouted into the radio set on the wall. 'Don't you have better devices for me? This scrap heap is obsolete.'
'No, the whole space ship is fit for scrap. I'm afraid we are too slow to reach our destination on time.'
'Hey, are you nuts? In half an hour we have to be on Enu. Many interested buyers are waiting there for the girls.'
'I don't think we'll be there on time', the voice from the loudspeaker replied.

'Ina!' Sesa cried out and wanted to run towards her sister, however the red eyed woman stopped her.
'She'll die!' Sesa screamed. 'She is from the planet Earth and she can't stand any flights in space ships!'
'Is that true?' Garos asked the robot.
'Yes. And presumably she can't stand the anesthetic either.'
'What? But you computed it, scrap heap!'
'It's too strong; an error. I erred with her body weight.'
'Erred? Is there anything you can do well?' Garos stared at the young terrestrial woman who was lying spread-eagled on the floor.
'Dry her off, put on her Quados, and cover her with a blanket. If she gets worse, notify me at once. Lysi, would you please come with me to the bridge?'
The red eyed woman looked at Garos with surprise and said in a deep voice: 'Darling, you can't leave the sisters alone with the robot!'
'Ina's unconscious and Sesa's bound. What can they do? And, furthermore, we are in a space ship in the open

space. They cannot jump out, can they?' Garos said smirking disdainfully at his girlfriend.
'You know exactly what I mean', she shouted at him. Her red eyes were glowing like fire, just like her pink-colored hair.
'Okay. I don't know what you're worrying about, but I'll get somebody to watch them.'
'That's good.'
A few seconds after Garos and Lysi had left the cargo compartment of the small space ship, two huge hairy monsters came to watch the sisters. Sesa was terrified because of the looks and the nauseating stench of the creatures. Nevertheless, the young Sathorjan girl dared to take a few steps towards her sister. The result was a loud growl and a paw blow throwing Sesa onto the ground. Sesa got back on her feet stumbling courageously toward her sister while she was crying: 'Wake up, please!'
As if she had heard Sesa crying for help, Ina began to move, and she opened her eyes only to see her sister being carried away by a huge pile of fur.
She tried to call Sesa, but couldn't utter a word.

'Hallo, my dear ones', Liess called out shuffling towards Farres' parents.
'Oh Liess! How are you?' Mula was delighted to greet the old lady giving her a warm welcome.
'I'm fine. It's wonderful to meet you here.' Kara and Zed warmly greeted the herbalist. She did a lot for Zed. She had given him essences to alleviate his pain and had always helped Mula and him. She even had given some good advice to Kara for her studies.
'Did Ina come back?' asked the old lady when she had sat down with the family.
'No', replied Farres.
'That's very strange. An hour ago I saw her when she was on her way to meet her sister on the corridor outside the toilets.

'This is a very strange meeting point', Kara said surprised.
'Well, I tried to contact them with the CC3 to ask if they needed help, but I could not establish any connection. Maybe I'm just an old fool and made a mistake operating the CC3.'
'Never mind; presumably they don't want to talk to anybody', Mula said conciliating.
'No, mother', Farres shouted alarmed. 'Rida sent a message to Ina saying that something terrible would happen during the festival. I was stupid enough not to take seriously the warning.' With a hand on his brow Farres tried to call Ina again, but in vain. 'They have been kidnapped', he stammered, and his face went pale.
'But that's impossible. Otherwise they would have given an alarm', Kara opined.
'I have no idea!' her brother said snorting.
'Maybe it's an act of sabotage?' Zed asked. 'Perhaps it has to do with the fact that Elsa and Chris showed up. I tell you: Somebody of the security department has a finger in that pie.'
'What? Losos?' Mula asked horrified. She didn't like the chief of the department, but she couldn't imagine him participating in abduction. It didn't make sense. He had wife and children, thus responsibilities.
'No, he's not the one. I rather think of somebody in charge of the maintenance of the computer systems.'
'There are several people involved in this', Farres said. He quickly communicated with security and notified the incident.

Ina heard Sesa's soft whimper. She herself was not strong enough to weep.
'What's going on?' a male voice asked the robot standing motionless beside Ina. The terrestrial woman didn't care much about them. She tried not to vomit at every single breath.

'She'll faint again soon.'
'Well, then do something about it!' Garos shouted. Ina couldn't stop him from touching her neck to feel her pulse. 'Damn!' he shouted angrily.
'What's the matter?' Zaq asked astonished. 'What's wrong with her?'

'Maybe she'll die before we have landed on Enu', Garos said with a sigh.
'Give her water', Zaq said hectically.
'Be sure we already did!' commented the lean guy annoyed. 'Who is the doctor here?'
'Yes, who is? I suppose you should be able to keep the girl alive until we can present her?' Zaq asked derisively. His round face was glaring red, and his short blonde hair stood on end pointing in all directions.
'Under these circumstances I prefer to dissect her myself', reasoned Garos.
'Hey, we have an agreement! You can't do that. Do you know how much money I owe?'
'I'm paying you more than enough', Garos replied coldly.
'And what about the half dozen people who think they have a share of the proceeds from Ina's sale?'
'That's nonsense! The experiment worked out perfectly, so these claims expired. This terrestrial woman brought up an amount of healing fruit for the next two years.'
'How do you know?'
'Somebody told me.'
'Who did?'
'I have my sources.' Garos was still looking at Ina. Meanwhile she had fallen unconscious again.
'Darling', commented Lysi. Her eyes were glowing dangerously. 'You promised something.'
'What do you want?' Garos asked impatiently.
'We're going to sell Ina and with that money we have a nice time together.'

Shivering and bleeding at her left shoulder Sesa sat in a corner and tried to listen to what they were talking about. She strained her ears, but she couldn't understand it all due to the pounding noise of the blood in her head.
'Okay, put her back into the water', Garos ordered the robot. 'I hope this will improve her blood circulation. At least Ronok said so.'
'A correct decision for once', Zaq commented and breathed a sigh of relief.

'Sesa and Ina have disappeared.' These words were a shock for the entire security department. Nuna turned around on her office chair looking from one to the other. Losos looked at her insistently. 'Error excluded?'
The young woman nodded: 'I have checked it all. Both girls are definitely not here anymore. Less than an hour ago a small space ship left the space port. Another one followed. Meanwhile more than ten space ships took off to return to their home planets.'
'All of them have been controlled?'
'Of course; so far there are no apparent abnormalities – just nothing.'
'On the surveillance photographs everything looks all right', a young assistant said.
'Have all the guests been checked when they left the planet?' Losos asked with a roaring voice.
'Yes, Sir', Nuna replied. She looked desperate. There had never been such a severe incident. The president's daughter had been kidnapped!
'Show me the photos!' Xio demanded. His wife leaned against his shoulder looking at the holograms building up in the air in front of them.
Minutes passed by without unusual occurrences.
'What is Zaq doing there?' Alons asked. 'I thought he was on service today.' In fact a small, corpulent man appeared for a moment standing in front of a space ship fit for scrap. On the following photos he wasn't there anymore.

'That's nothing unusual', said Losos. 'He bought that space ship a couple of days ago. He wants to repair it to go on excursions when he retires from service.'
'Isn't Zaq in charge of the computer maintenance?' Farres asked.
'Yes, he is', Losos confirmed.
'Couldn't he have manipulated the system?'
'Pardon me?' Losos looked at Farres as if he had gone mad.
'Yes', Alons reasoned. 'Lately he has been behaving strangely; almost always he's working alone. I tell you, that's part of a sophisticated plan.'
'And Rida, too', his brother said.
'Don't be absurd!' Nuna said. 'Which motive could she have?'
'Jealousy; she wants to get rid of Ina and threatened her several times.'
Those threats just were insignificant messages on a CC3', Xio commented. 'That doesn't help us at all.'

'Is it true?' Ronok shouted throughout the security department. Liess had told him about the disappearance of the two sisters.
'Yes, it is', Losos said bitterly. 'Sesa and Ina were kidnapped. The incident with their parents was part of the plan. Our security system was infiltrated.'
'How long ago did this happen?' Ronok asked.
'More than an hour ago.'
'They'll want to sell the girls', the doctor supposed. Bora moaned loudly.
'We have to do something!' Farres shouted upset.
'And what can we do? Detain Zaq just because he has bought a space ship and is flying around with it?' Nuna asked derisively. 'There's no evidence, neither against Zaq nor against Rida. Even if her parents had bought the space ship for Zaq...'

'That's it!' Alons said. 'Where did he get all that money for a space ship from?'
'Okay, Alons, you have to check immediately Zaq's finances and Rida's family's, too. Maybe you can find out something suspicious.'
'This will take its time', said Alons. 'They'll have transferred the money non-obviously. I'll have to make a special effort to find out.'
Alons went to his working place.
They played the surveillance video again. Zaq was clearly visible, but there was also another man talking to him for a fleeting moment.
'Who is this?' Xio wondered all of a sudden. 'I know that man!'
'That's Garos', Ronok stated.
'He's not your fellow student, is he?' Losos asked.
'Yes, he is.'
'Wasn't that the guy we had to escort out of the palace some time ago?'
'That's right. For a long time he has been trying to disclose the secret of my experiment', Ronok said anxiously.
'Pardon me?' Farres was getting excited. 'You are just concerned about your experiment. I'm worried about what he's going to do to Ina!' He was exasperated looking at Ronok like a predator at his prey. 'How could you do this to Ina?'
'No one could have predicted this development', Ronok said firmly. 'Do you seriously think that I'm happy about it? All my research in recent years…'
'You only think of your research, nothing else', Farres shouted enraged. 'What about Ina? She is somewhere out there with an insane guy who has only one purpose, and that is to dissect her!'
'Farres, calm down!' Losos looked angrily at the young man. 'This won't help, especially not Ina.'
'How could Garos get into the building?' Xio asked the security people.

'As a guest like all the others, too', said Losos sighing.
'Everything was done legally. Zaq invited Garos together with a group of people to the great festival', Nuna explained.
'They lured Sesa out of the hall on some false pretense. Then Ina followed her sister; this was easy to foresee. The security system has been paralyzed before, as were the girls' CC3s.' Losos declared.
'Well, it was easy to abduct Sesa and Ina in the chaos created by Elsa and Chris' appearance', commented Alons.
'By the way, Rida's parents have transferred money to Zaq.'
'So he's our main suspect.' Losos sighed. He was profoundly shaken by the fact that his friend and colleague had been able to do such a thing.
'Just a moment', Nuna cried out turning pale. 'I remember now! Zaq has recently loaded new software on the host computer and…' she went on with a quivering voice.
'A virus?' Xio looked from one face to the other.
'That's quite possible', Losos said. He sighed again. 'I never thought Zaq would take part in such a thing.'
'How long are you going to wait', Farres shouted enraged. 'We have to start the search for that space ship at once!'
'That's true; time is pressing', said Ronok.
'Try to find out where that scrap shuttle went. Put together a task force and get the transformation robots ready!' Xio cast a look at his motionless wife and said firmly:
'Of course Bora and I are coming along, too.'
'That's too dangerous', Nuna said quickly.
'I can't sit back here and take things easy, while my daughter is in danger!'
Fifteen minutes later, a space ship left Sathorja with course to Enu. It had been easy to trace Zaq's space ship.

Cool air entered Ina's lungs. First she had no idea of her terrible situation. She heard lots of voices without knowing who they belonged to. Still half asleep she tried to turn around to adopt a more comfortable position, but this was impossible. Her wrists and ankles hurt like hell when she tried to move. She opened her eyes and wished she hadn't. She was lying on a cold disk floating in the air. Her wrists and ankles were tied with strange, glowing slings of orange color immobilizing her completely. Countless human and alien eyes were looking at her.
'She is awake', somebody grunted.
In the beginning Ina didn't know how to react; she only hoped she was dreaming and hadn't awoken yet. Slowly she began to remember: The festival, her parents, and the flight in the space ship. All these curious onlookers just wanted to know what her body was like, and how she was able to breath under water. Her death seemed to be inescapable. Ina had to get away from here; desperately she tried to free herself. But the bonds cut painfully into her wrists. Suddenly from the corner of her eye she saw something pointy and sharp flashing in the dazzling light. She began to scream, hence somebody covered her mouth. Sesa yelled her name.
Seconds later Ina felt a horrible pain piercing her body; she fell unconscious again.
Sesa was horror-stricken staring at Ina. Her gills were bleeding. Garos and several others had begun their deadly work. Sesa had to watch while they were dissecting her elder sister alive.

Xio stood in front of the small, old space ship they had found abandoned on a rocky plateau somewhere on the dwarf planet Enu. 'Where have they gone?' he asked astonished.
The arid surroundings gave no indication for the place where the kidnappers could have brought the sisters.
'There's no trace of them', stated a TFR.
'They can't have vanished into thin air', Farres said sighing. 'What about subterranean caves?'
'That's ridiculous', commented Nuna with a disdainful look at Farres. 'There's only massive rock hundreds of yards deep. There's nothing underneath. We have checked it all.'
'That doesn't matter. You have to search the whole area', Losos ordered. 'Tunia?'
'I have understood', she replied. 'I'll convince the other TFRs to participate in the search.'
'What? We are combat robots', complained one of the male TFRs. a minute later. 'Our field of responsibilities does not include a search.'
'Just do it!' Xio shouted at him. 'I can also give the order to transfer you or to melt you down!'
Farres was running over the mighty stone slabs looking for gaps and cracks in the rocks. He became careless, lost his footing, and slid a couple of yards downhill. Immediately he got back on his feet and looked around.
'What are you doing there?' Alons asked his brother. 'Hey, what's that? It looks like a hatch!'
Farres looked down and saw that he was standing exactly on a greyish-green door.
'Come here!' Alons called waving his hands. 'Farres has found the entrance.'
Xio was the first one to reach the two young men. 'Come up here, Farres!'
'I'll try', replied Farres and started to climb uphill, but he slipped and landed on that door again. 'I can't get out of here! You'll have to help me.'

Finally one of the transformation robots heaved Farres up to the rocky plateau.
'We'll take over now', said Tunia. 'TFRs and taskforce ready to intervene.'
Everybody knew what that meant.
'Intervention!' Losos commanded.

After several minutes Ina regained consciousness. Somebody was trying to give her water squirting it down her throat so that she almost choked. Her situation hadn't changed. She was still lying face down on that strange, cool disk. She didn't try to free herself anymore. Any attempt was impossible due to the excruciating pain flooding her body.
A deep roar made the subterranean hall tremble. Garos ceased to work and looked around. Unrest spread in the hideaway.
'Don't panic!' somebody shouted.
Several minutes elapsed. Garos devoted himself to Ina again.
'Please don't!' Ina begged scarcely audible. But there was no compassion. Again a searing pain flashed through her powerless body before she lost consciousness.
Once more the hall was shaken to its very foundations.
'We have been discovered' Lysi screamed and pointed to a strange halo of light high up near the entrance hatch.
'Calm down, darling', replied Garos. 'We are prepared for everything.'
'Are we?'
'There is a system of escape tunnels.'
'Then we should quickly disappear', Lysi gasped.
'It's a pity!' Garos cast a last look at Ina.
'You've gathered enough information about Ina', his girlfriend said annoyed, gripped his arm, and made him follow her.
'Maybe you're right, but I couldn't uncover the secret completely. The time was too short.'

He quickly followed the red eyed woman through the increasing chaos.

'That's my Dad', Sesa murmured after a further rumble. She got up on her feet looking at the bright spot on the ceiling spreading quickly. Zaq shook his head while he was trying to push up the price for Sesa to astronomical heights.
'Look at her! Isn't she pretty?' he asked the crowd interiorly nervous, but with an engaging smile on his face. 'And she's young!'
'Xio would do anything to get her back', remarked a chubby woman. 'We could blackmail him. I always wished to know what life in the palace is like and…'
'Darling, are you crazy? He would hunt us down with his entire army', commented the corpulent man at her side.
'That's nonsense!'
'Let it be!' The man pulled his mate away from Sesa.
'Well, who is offering more?' Zaq asked. 'No one's offering more? Well, my dear friend, Sesa is yours.' An extremely lean creature paid Zaq a large amount of money, gripped Sesa's arm, and led her to his equals who visibly showed their appreciation.
Zaq was rubbing his hands. He could be content, but now it was time to disappear as quickly as possible.
Suddenly the hall went dark. There were screams, trampling, and panic.
'We are being attacked!' an anxious female voice cried out.
'To the escape tunnels!' somebody shouted.
Zaq had expected the attack of the Sathorjan troops, although not so soon. His escape from Enu was well prepared. He knew that they would use TFRs, and those robots always attacked in the dark. In case that this happened, he had brought a night-vision device and strolled comfortably through the panicking crowd towards one of the nearby exits. Garos didn't bother him. They business

relation ended today, as did the relation with Rida's parents. They had served him well, as had the pilots and part of the crew. He would transfer them the payment they had agreed upon. From Garos he had received a large sum for Ina, so there was nothing left to do on this desolate celestial body.

The Sathorjan task force and the TFRs entered the hall under cover of darkness. They came in virtual silence maneuvering the attendees into one corner by force of arms. Everything went according to plan; two minutes later the room was bathed in dazzling light, but suddenly an entire robot army was marching up. All at once Sesa and Ina were in midst of the skirmish. Sesa had taken advantage of the dark and run away from the lean creature. Now she was stumbling toward her sister who was half dead and hardly perceived the events around her.
'Ina!' cried Sesa, when a robot of the enemy army seized her. Ina made an effort turning her head only to see Sesa trying desperately to worm her way out of the machine's grip. Oh, my God! Ina could hardly believe her eyes. What was that huge monster that rescued Sesa from the machine's clutches? That giant thing was carrying Sesa on one arm while it was running towards Ina by long leaps. Ina tried not to look, but she had to. She was staring at a metallic monster more than ten feet tall.
'Ina', Sesa called, when the mighty machine put her down next to her sister. Then it spread a net of blue laser rays over the two young women.
'Stay with your sister', a soft female voice said. The machine stood still for a couple of seconds – Ina could feel its look directed at her – and then it disappeared.
'What is it?' Ina whispered in amazement.
'That's a TFR, Ina. Everything is going to be okay!' Sesa whispered nearly inaudibly. Cautiously she loosened the fetters of Ina's wrists and ankles. 'They'll get us out of here soon.

Ina answered with a slight blinking of her eyes as she was incapable of doing any more.

'Where are they?' Losos asked over his CC3.
'In the rear section of the hall', Tri, the chief of the task force, explained. 'It's difficult to get them out there because…'
'Why?' cried Xio in the background.
'An army of enemy robots is intervening in the conflict.'
'Pardon me?' Losos couldn't believe it.
'And there's more! They are outnumbering our forces.'
'I don't understand this', Xio said panting with rage. 'There are no armed forces on the planet Enu. Who do they belong to? Certainly not to Zaq and that Garos.'
'Someone with great power has a finger in the pie', Alons remarked.
'That's true', Tri confirmed Alons' words. 'You are not safe anymore on the rocky plateau. We don't know who's controlling this robot army, and whom we are dealing with. This might be an attack against you being the president of the United Planets.'
'Pardon me?' Xio asked. 'Do you think we've fallen into a trap?'
'That's possible. You must return immediately to Sathorja! Otherwise the interplanetary peace will be endangered!'
'No!' Bora cried out. 'We can't leave Sesa alone!'
'My unit is doing its best to save Sesa and Ina.' The call had ended.
'But you heard Tri. We can't stay here!' Xio looked desperately at his weeping wife.
'Sesa needs us!' Bora said sobbing.
'Do we have any information about my daughter?' Xio asked in suspense.
'Yes', replied Ronok. 'Tunia sent me all the medical data of both girls. Sesa is injured, but it's nothing serious.'
'What about Ina?' Farres wanted to know.

The doctor looked into the young man's eyes and said slowly: 'She is seriously hurt.'
'How serious is it?' Farres inquired.
'Her interior bleedings are very serious; without help she won't survive the next hour.'
Ronok's face gave nothing away, but he was terribly enraged that his experiment had been willfully destroyed. The fact that poor innocent Ina had been tortured so much that she was dying down there now, affected him more than he would like to admit.
'No!' cried Farres. He staggered backward, ran his fingers through his black hair and looked desperately from one to the other.
'We have to help her', he whispered with a husky voice.
'That's impossible', said Losos firmly. 'Xio, listen to Tri and fly back to Sathorja with your wife!'
'It's too late!' Nuna said panicking. 'They have already discovered us.' She pointed to a group of robots rapidly approaching them.
'Damn!' Losos cried. 'We have no choice. We have to go down into the hall! Only there you can be protected, Xio.' As quickly as possible, Losos contacted the chief of the task force. 'We are coming down to you!'
'You can't be serious!' the voice on the other end of the line said. 'You don't know what is going on down here.'
'Up here it's not any better. Enemy robots are approaching us', Losos shouted into his device. 'We are entirely unprotected. Send us a TFR to the entrance hatch, so he can protect the president!'
Shortly afterwards a TFR opened the hatch.
'Bring me to my daughter at once!' Xio ordered the machine.

'Stay with me, Ina!' Sesa wept. She held her sister's head with both hands. Ina had closed her eyes and breathed heavily. Blood was oozing out of her sides. In some places her skin had adopted a bluish tint. 'Please! I need you!'

Ina was fighting with all her strength against her body's need to fall unconscious. She sensed that she was close to death. She felt an icy cold even though in the subterranean hall the temperature had to be at least 25 degrees. Soon she would face her creator.
'Darling!' Farres voice penetrated deeply into her befuddled consciousness. Was she dreaming? She tried desperately to release herself from the clutches of the approaching death and to react.
'Ina!' She heard Farres calling her again. Somehow she achieved to return into today's reality. It was tremendously comforting to have a boyfriend. The fact that Ronok was also there, didn't affect her. Maybe he could help her.
The painkiller Ronok dribbled into her mouth did her good, and the words he said to her were even more astonishing: 'Ina, I am heartily sorry for what has happened to you.' Compassionately he was stroking her head. 'You are safe now. Nobody will do you any harm.'
Ina looked at him for a moment, and then she closed her eyes.
'You can help her, can't you?' Farres asked appalled.
'Yes, if I get a TFR to assist me.'

'What can we do now?' Nuna asked. The hall looked like a battle field and it was clear that the Sathorjan unit was pulling back more and more. Soon all the TFRs and the entire combat unit were kept busy just by protecting the president and his family.
'Wait and see', Alons said coldly. Nuna was getting on his nerves; he disliked her arrogance. Furthermore, it hurt him to see his brother sitting beside his seriously hurt girlfriend suffering helplessly.
Sesa clang to her mother. She wished to be embraced like a little baby. Bora was visibly relieved to get her daughter back practically unharmed and enjoyed the moment. Xio looked at his wife and daughter with mixed feelings.

What did he have to expect? Who was the author of that devilish plan?
A man in uniform thronged through the defense line formed around the Sathorjan group. 'We have to surrender, Xio. We are outnumbered; our people can impossibly fight against one hundred robots. The most important thing for the moment is to protect you and your family.'
'Did anybody claim responsibility for this?' Xio asked increasingly nervous.
'We don't know any names, but a few minutes ago a message arrived saying they want to negotiate with you personally, if you are prepared to do so.'
Xio looked around worriedly. The TFRs had secured the Sathorjans with a protective laser grille, even though this protection consumed lots of energy. How long would they be able to persevere?
Ronok approached him and said insistently: 'I need Tunia; otherwise I can't help Ina.'
'Damn!' Losos had listened and groaned. 'Tri, we need Tunia. Send her to Ina!'
'Hey, are you crazy?' the chief nagged. 'All the TFRs are indispensable. Our defense depends on them.'
'Ina is dying', Ronok said.
'If we're not careful, all of us will die', Tri replied furiously.
I'm going to negotiate', Xio said with embitterment, 'so you can pull off Tunia and send her over to us.'
Ina's eyes widened when she saw the TFR approaching her. A tremor flashed through her agonized body.
'Tunia, could you please transform yourself? Ina is afraid of you', Farres asked, when Tunia arrived.
'Pardon me', she said with her soft voice, 'but at the moment it's not possible.'
'Ina', Ronok turned to the terrestrial, 'I know you're afraid of Tunia, but please be brave. Calm down and concentrate on Farres.'

How should she do that? A metallic giant monster right beside her, and she wasn't allowed to get excited. Tears of despair were burning in her eyes. 'Ina, you can do it', Ronok said compassionately. 'Is there any way to distract Ina a little?' he asked.
'Maybe something from her home planet would help', Alons reflected.
'You are really crazy', Nuna said disdainfully. 'We can't carry things from other planet with us.'
'Tunia, play some music from Earth for Ina!' Farres' order caused a general disconcertment.
'She's not a radio!' Losos cried angrily.
'No problem', the machine replied. Immediately Ina heard soft classical music – melodies she hadn't heard for a long time.
'Can't you switch of that tootling?' Nuna groaned. 'We already have enough problems.'
'Ina relaxes', Tunia commented.
And a little later Bora said: 'And Sesa too.'

'Wow, you must really love your terrestrial girls if you listen to this horrible music', said a deep voice. A small creature thronged his way through the Sathorjans.
'Who are you?' Xio asked. A small man with big grey eyes looked at him deprecatingly. A TFR had positioned beside Xio to protect him, and also the soldiers viewed him with suspicion.
'Your enemy', the creature replied. His green body hair bristled with every word. The uniform he wore was much too big for him and made him look even smaller.
'What do you want?' Xio asked icily.
'Freedom for my people.'
'Have you got anything to do with the abduction of my daughter?' Xio looked furiously at the little man.
'Depends on how you look at it. I just made this hall available to Zaq.'
Xio panted furiously.

'I wonder if all of you are as naïve as that guy Zaq. He really thought I wouldn't expect anything in return. He just was a piece of puzzle of my plan.'
'You!' Xio gasped.
'Calm down! At the moment Zaq is sitting together with Garos, the sweet red eyed woman and the furry monsters in a jail cell in the rocks. By the way, my name is Qop.'
'Why are you doing all this?' Losos asked exasperatedly.
'For a long time I wanted to talk to the president personally. Do you know how many times I have already been rejected?'
Xio looked at Qop and said icily: 'Under these circumstances I don't want to listen to you. First you have to release my family and my people.'
'Do you really think you can impose conditions?' Qop snarled. His lush-green hair bristled. 'You are in my power. I could start any time to kill you one by one. I think that young woman over there will be the first victim you'll have to mourn.'
The little man pointed to Nuna who stared at him stricken with fear.
'If that doesn't help, it's your terrestrial girl's turn. Garos certainly will want to finish his job.'
Xio wiped the sweat from his brow.
'And if you don't mind this either, I'll devote to your daughter.'
'No', Xio shouted enraged, when Qop scuttled a few steps towards Sesa.
'What do you want me to do?' he asked.
'Well, I want the delegates of the United Planets pass a law assuring my people can return to their home planet. Until then you can consider yourself as my guests.'
Xio shook his head. 'You are crazy. How can I do that? Do you think I'm almighty? I don't even know your people.'
'As you see', scolded the little man, 'you don't even know that we exist, because we have to live on this horrible moon in the subsurface!' His green face turned black

and his eyes shone turquoise blue. The size of his body changed; he grew steadily until he was a head taller than Xio. The TFR reacted at once and pointed a weapon at the creature.

'Tell your robot not to do that! One simple gesture of my hand and your daughter's dead.'

Xio signaled the TFR to pull back.

'Give me a couple of minutes to discuss the issue with my people.'

'Okay, but I'm afraid you have no choice anyway. My robot army is numerically superior; my people are living directly under this hall in an extensive cave system of this damned moon and can join us if necessary.'

'Why do you stay on Enu, if you don't like it?' asked Alons in astonishment.

Enu was one of the most inhospitable moons of the water planet. It just consisted of different classes of rock, had hardly any vegetation, and its climate was really horrible – cold and rainy.

'Why do you ask?' Qop asked in a barking voice. 'We have been exiled here by force many years ago. The planetary federation wanted to use our planet as a raw material supplier so now it's forbidden to live there. We simply were relocated by force.' The creature paused for breath, and then it said: 'On Enu we have to live under the ground, hence our people are threatened with extinction. We need the sun and not darkness, so the mortality rate is extremely high! But no matter how often I have made applications to the council or wished to talk to the president I have always been rejected.'

What's the name of your home planet?' Losos asked tensely.

'Gito.'

'No!' Losos panted in horror. 'That was your home?'

This planet had served for many years to supply the raw materials needed for the manufacturing of the construction material Ips.

Ina listened to the music and had forgotten about her surroundings. Thanks to the analgesic, the pain kept within a limit. Obediently she took further medicaments and also achieved to drink some water. Farres stayed at her side and caressed her head tenderly while he was listening attentively to the odd alien's words.
'Let my family and my people return to Sathorja. I'll stay here as your hostage', declared Xio.
'Oh, the self-sacrificing statesman! Delightful. What will the delegates say?' Qop commented smirking. Suddenly he got serious. 'The president used as leverage. We'll see if the majority is on your side, or they just let you kick the bucket here.'
'Xio, you can't do that', Losos cried insistently. 'This will undermine your position of power. It would appear as a sign of weakness.'
'That doesn't matter', Xio quietly said. 'I want to make sure you are safe.'
'But you are essential for the cohesion of the planetary community', Losos replied. 'Without you the federation is endangered!'
'If I don't return, a new president will be elected. He'll care for the continuity of the federation.'
'Xio is saving our lives', Nuna rejoiced happily.
Suddenly there was an uncomfortable silence. It was as if nobody dared to breathe. Only the terrestrial music was flowing out of Tunia's interior.
'Well', Qop began to say pathetically, 'you shall have your hero! Apart from the president everybody is allowed go back to the space ship.'
'Darling!' Bora screamed appalled. She let Sesa go and ran toward Xio. 'Please, don't let us alone!' Sesa ran behind her mother screaming with a weeping voice: 'I'm terribly sorry! It was entirely my fault. I shouldn't have run away!'
'Oh no!' said the little man. 'I would have brought you to Enu anyway to be able to seize your father, no matter

under whatsoever pretext.'
'Qop please, let me talk to my family for a moment!' Xio asked looking stonily.
Qop shook his head. He signaled two of his robots to lead Xio off. Then he prompted his army to retreat.
'Wait', Losos called the green creature, 'what will happen, when the delegates don't agree with your plan?'
'Then I'll have to kill your president, and sent him well packed to Sathorja. Afterwards I shall be forced to choose a new victim until my wish is accepted.'
Bora fell on her knees before Qop. She was weeping bitterly. 'Please release my husband. You don't need a hostage. The delegates will agree with your wish anyway.'
'To believe this is very naïve. Unfortunately in this case I can't achieve my aim without the use of force.'
Bora looked powerlessly at Qop. Sesa helped her to get on her feet, supporting and comforting her. She felt tremendously guilty.
Tri shook his head despondently. 'That was not exactly Xio's masterpiece. He could have saved himself and request reinforcement. Our army would have destroyed this green critter and his people.'
'Pardon me!' said Alons. 'Before Qop would have made his robots kill us all!'
'You're talking nonsense as always', Nuna replied.
'Really? You would have been the first to die!' he commented cynically.
'Alons, now the United Planets are without a president. You don't understand the impact of what Xio did. It may have been good for us, but not for our community.'
'That's right', said Losos. 'Xio should have borne in mind the effects of his actions.'
After a short break Nuna asked: 'What happens with Zaq and the others?'
'That doesn't really matter now', replied Losos.
'Folks', said Tri to everybody, 'we have to get away from this damned moon at once!'

'That's right', somebody shouted impatiently. 'If Xio sacrifices himself, at least it shouldn't have been in vain.'
'Well, then let's return home', said Losos. 'Is Ina fit for transport?' he asked Ronok.
'We'll be able to bring her to the space ship, but I'm not sure she'll survive the journey home.'
'You can't be serious?'
'Yes, I am. Ina is already much weakened. The flight here was a tremendous exertion for her, and then she wasn't injured.'
'Well, then give her an anesthetic', Tri cried angrily.
'I can't do that without putting her life in danger', replied Ronok. 'On the flight here she has already been given a strong anesthetic. As long as there's still part of it in her blood, I can't give her another dose.'
'How long do we have to wait?' Losos asked.
'About an hour.'
'We can't take this into consideration', remarked Tri.
'What did you say?' Farres asked enraged. He had stood up and was looking alternately at Tri and at Losos.
'Your friend is not the only passenger', replied Tri coldly. 'We don't know if these people are preparing another surprise for us.'
'I don't think so', commented Losos. 'Moreover, in the space ship we'll be reasonably safe. We can wait there.'
Sesa looked at Losos with surprise. She hadn't thought he would show so much humaneness.
'You'll be held responsible!' Tri shouted furiously.
'That's right', said Losos. 'Xio is not here anymore, so I am in charge now. I'll decide in accordance with his intentions, do you understand?'
'You'll endanger us all!' a woman shouted wrathfully.
'There are no indications for it', Losos said coldly.
More than an hour later the Sathorjan space ship eventually left the inhospitable moon Enu. Without any more problems and incidents they returned to Sathorja.

Xio was sitting in an obscure cell. It was situated under the hall and quite austere. He was all alone; the Gitoans hadn't considered it necessary to guard him. Anyway, where could he go?

How long would he have to stay in this dungeon? Would the delegates give in to the demand of that green creature at all? Wouldn't the economic interests be more important? Was there any possible solution? Xio did not only have friends in the council; some of them begrudged his position and would like to replace him. What would happen to Zaq and the others? Qop had them in his power; hopefully he'd make them suffer a bit. Incredible what Zaq had done to him! He would pay for it. Somehow Xio had to achieve to call him to account for Ina's cruel agony. After all, the terrestrial girl was Sesa's sister! Oh Sesa! Xio began to think of his beloved wife and daughter. When he held Sesa in his arms for the first time, his family's happiness seemed perfect. How quickly had Sesa become a young lady! The years had gone by too fast. She was stubborn; always crushing her head against a brick wall. But Sesa was a good daughter!

And then he had to think about something else: What should he do with Elsa and Chris? He couldn't send them back to that desolate planet; this would break Sesa's heart. Maybe he should allow them to live in his palace. They couldn't do much harm. With those new CC3s Sesa and Ina's parents could be perfectly supervised. If someday he would be able to hug his family again. Silent desperation invaded his soul. Eventually, haunted by nightmares, he fell asleep.

'Oh no', Maris sighed. 'What have they done to her?'
'To me it looks damaged beyond repair', concluded Okon. 'We should remove the complete gill tissue and thus enable Ina to lead a normal life. After this incident she will appreciate it.'
'I don't agree with you', replied Ronok. 'We can restore her gills.'
'How?' Ana asked. 'Do you know how many difficult operations will be necessary to do that? In this state she won't survive it.'
'She will. Make all the necessary preparations!'
'Darling, just think it over again. Ina has suffered a lot and…'
'Maris, I know what I can inflict on her.'

'Tell your people, they have three days', said Qop, the Citoan. He was standing in his original small size in front of Xio and put a little device into his hand.
'An ultimatum?' Xio asked. 'That's impossible. Some of the delegates need more than a day to get to Sathorja.'
'Do they have to appear in person on Sathorja?' Qop asked.
'Of course.' Xio panted.
'That's not my problem. Don't lose the time. You know what happens, if they don't comply with my ultimatum.'
Xio nodded and called the security department.
'What?' Losos asked exasperated. 'Only three days? That's almost impossible. We have to inform all the re-

presentatives of the planets and all the nations entitled for vote.'
'I know, my old friend!' Xio sighed.
'I won't let you down. I'll do my best to get you out safe and sound.'
'Thank you!' Xio said powerlessly.

The days went by. Short before the ultimatum expired, the delegates gathered in the small hearing room.
'No, that's out of question', a female voice boomed. 'We depend on the raw materials from Gito.'
'You are risking the president's life!' somebody said excitedly.
'He should have kept a better eye on his daughter', another one said.
'Silence!' shouted the chairman and looked around wrathfully. One or two representatives of each planet of the federation had come. Forty four people took part in the conference, many shouting at the same time. Supporters and opponents quickly became evident. There had often been disputes in the hall. It was modest and convenient. Comfortable sofas were floating a few inches above the floor around an illuminated podium. The feeble light of the evening suns streaming through the huge windows made it glow warmly – quite contrary to the ice cold debates just being under way…
'Xio knew exactly what he was getting involved with', declared Tri.
He had to appear as a witness and describe the incident down to the smallest detail.
'Where are the terrestrials Elsa and Chris at the moment?' an elderly lady asked.
'What has this got to do with the incident on Enu?' The chairman asked.
'They are in custody in the palace', Losos said quickly. He hated deliberations, all the more so when a friend's life was at stake.

'For Xio his family is more important than the planetary community's welfare', somebody shouted loudly.
'No', somebody else contradicted him. 'He has actually saved our people. Those Gitoans would have executed one after the other.'
'We don't negotiate with terrorists', said a very old creature with a booming voice.
Turmoil arose.
'Silence or I order to clear the hall!' the chairman shouted.
The hall calmed down at once.
'Please allow me to say something', Bora called into the silence.
Well, please step up!' said the chairman and motioned her over to him.
'Maybe my husband didn't act like a politician, but like a father. He wanted to save our Sesa who had been abducted from Sathorja. I admit that this mission might have endangered the unity, however he achieved to bring us back home safe and sound. He sacrificed himself for his people.' Tears were running down Bora's cheeks. 'Maybe I'll never see him again, and Sesa has to grow up without a father.'
Somebody gave her a handkerchief, so she could wipe off the tears. 'Thank you for your attention', she said in a faltering voice.
Murmurs filled the room. Bora was weeping while she stepped down from the podium.
An official expert in the issue went to the podium: 'I'd like to explain quickly, what a solution for Gito might be like.
'Do we really have to listen to this mindless drivel?' an attractive woman cried out loudly. 'Our entire building industry depends on the raw materials from this planet!'
'Let him state the facts!' said the chairman icily.
The presentation dragged on at length. The interest of the attendees diminished gradually, some of them already yarned. Eventually the expert concluded: 'As you

see there's a solution for everything. We give back their home planet to the Gitoans, but they are only allowed to live on it in certain areas.'
'What happens if there are too many people?' somebody asked.
'They have been decimated by the wars', said an elderly, wise man. 'In those days hundreds of thousands have died when they tried to defend their planet. The last conflict was about seventy years ago, and their population has not yet recovered.'
'Let's vote!' said the chairman after a brief pause.

On the third day Xio was staring without emotion at his breakfast, when Qop walked into his cell. He was accompanied by an equally green and hairy female creature who was smiling at Xio in a gruesome way. Her black teeth were sparkling between her green lips, and her grey eyes were staring at him.
'Have you come to kill me?' Xio said sighing. 'I am prepared.'
'No, we'll sent you back to your family safe and sound', Qop declared.
Xio jumped up. He looked at the two in surprise.
'Yeah, in a couple of days we'll be able to return to Gito. My wife will give birth to our child on our home planet.' He pointed to the small brioche of his wife.
'Really?' Xio asked astonished. In fact, the majority of the delegates had opted for the Gitoans' homecoming. This was incredible. He hadn't expected this in his boldest dreams.
'You will be brought to Sathorja as soon as all of us have returned to Gito.'
'How long will that take?'
'Well, just a couple of days. They say our resettlement has the highest priority. Many space shuttles will come to take us and our belongings to Gito. As soon as we arrive there safely, you'll be brought to Sathorja.'

'Where are you going to live?' Xio asked confused.
'We'll live temporarily in provisional dwellings; however I have obtained the consent for the construction of modern housing estates.'
'This is unbelievable', Xio commented perplexed. 'Your people get a new chance.'
'Yes, thanks to you! By the way, I wouldn't have killed anyone of your people, nor you. I just played a little bit of theatre. We Gitoans are peace-loving people, you know?'
'However, you have arranged the kidnapping of my daughter', Xio stated angrily.
'Perhaps. But you won't be able to prove it. All the traces have been wiped out. But there is evidence against Zaq.'
'What will happen to him?'
'I'll hand him over to you. I don't need him anymore.'
'And the others?'
'Well, I'll have to set free that crazy guy who almost killed your amphibious girl and his red eyed girlfriend as well. The rest of Zaq's crew will be brought to Hedoncus.' Qop laughed happily. When Xio looked at him with surprise, he explained: 'They belong to a group of petty criminals wanted for a long time.'
'It's a pity that you can't detain them all. You'd save me much work.'
'Who is the president?' the green creature asked smirking. Xio shook his head.
'Now it's time to say good bye', said Qop a little later. 'I'm leaving Enu in an hour. Give my best regards to your very charming daughter, her amphibious sister and your wife.'

Four days later a space ship picked up Xio and brought him home to Sathorja. He couldn't believe it.
When he went from the space port to the palace, he slowly began to realize that he was free again. He took a transporter to his flat. It was a moment of great joy when he met his wife and his daughter again and could hug them!

'Why did the delegates vote in favor of Qop?' he asked his wife during supper.

'Well, I think it was because of you, darling. The majority of the representatives of the planetary community didn't want to lose their president. Moreover, many of them understand your behavior; especially those who have kids.'

Bora kissed her husband on his brow and said smiling: 'Welcome home. It's wonderful that you're back.'

Far away she heard soft music gently waking her up from a deep, restful sleep. Sluggishly she opened her eyes. She was in the laboratory again, but that wasn't a surprise. However, she didn't quite understand why she was listening to her favorite Beatles' song. She looked around wondering where the music came from. On a little floating table to her right next to a water container there was a small luminous pyramid. Did the music come from there? Ina tried to grasp it, but it was too far away. Tediously she moved a bit to the right and took the object cautiously with both hands. It was flickering in a bluish light, and then an orange color light spread over its surfaces. At the same time the device became warmer and the music louder. The Beatles sang 'Let it be', and it became even louder. She wanted to put back the pyramid onto its place. But it slipped out of her hands and fell down on the floor. That made the music fall silent at once. Exhausted Ina fell back onto her bed.

'What's that noise?' Ronok shouted angrily. He focused the pyramid – meanwhile it had turned deep blue. He picked it up putting it back on the table.

'How are you, dear?' he asked Ina compassionately while he sat down at her side.

Ina shied away from him.

'Don't be afraid of me, Ina. You should know.' He put his cool hand on her forehead and said: 'Close your eyes and breathe deeply. Everything will be all right. Trust me!'

Ina stared at him as if he were out of his mind.

'You are safe', he went on. He caressed her head softly and talked to her calming her down. Eventually Ina gave in, closed her eyes and calmed down indeed.
'That's good', she heard Ronok say. 'Listen to me. What happened on Enu will never happen again.'
Ina had to think of Garos placidly cutting tissues out of her body. And of the aliens cruelly trying to discover the secret of her gill breathing.
'I know that it hurts you much to remember these horrible things', Ronok said caringly. 'Do you want to talk about it?'
Ina shook her head.
'Hereafter nobody will dare to do you any harm. Soon you'll be a citizen of the United Planets.'
'But…' Ina began confused.
'I've granted freedom to you as a present. Xio will try to obtain the permission of the council for your adoption.'
'Pardon me?' Ina stammered.
'You'll become Xio and Bora's daughter. It's the only way to protect you and keep you safe.'
Ina swallowed. At first no parents, and now she had two fathers and two mothers?
'I'd like to ask you to stay here at the lab for a couple of days, so I can take care of you until you are fit again. You have suffered horrible things. You are very weak and need to rest urgently.'
Ina didn't say a word for a while; then she asked timidly: 'Will I be able to breathe under the water again?'
'Yes, but it'll take several weeks, until you can dive as usual again.'
For a moment Ina's eyes lit up. 'Thank you', she whispered.
'Don't mention it', Ronok said and caressed her hair peaceably. Then he took the pyramid and put it into Ina's hands. 'Tunia recorded music from our two last missions to the planet Earth on this device. You can easily operate it just by touching it.'

Indeed, in her hands the pyramid became warm and began to play music.
'You can adjust the volume with your fingers; a slight pressure lowers the volume, and if you press strongly, it gets louder. You can choose the songs by thinking of them; I think that's no problem for you.'
Ina was fascinated. This little distraction was good for her.
'One more thing', Ronok said severely, 'don't play your strange music too loudly.'
Ina nodded. She thought for a moment and then she asked a strange question: 'Ronok, could you please care for Zed?'
'Pardon me?'
'Farres' father, you know. He is ill, and Alons said I should ask you', Ina stammered timidly. She already wanted to ask the doctor earlier to help Zed, but she hadn't had the courage to do so. But now this had changed.
'Of course', Ronok said friendly and left the laboratory.

'Ina, this is really impressing!' said the old Sathorjan lady putting a tray with Ina's favorite food on the little table beside her bed. Ina turned to Liess and put the pyramid back on its place. The device switched off immediately.
'You can leave it on. This music is wonderful!'
The program had arrived at baroque piano music. She was listening to Mozart and Bach.
'On the planet Earth they seem to have a better musical taste than here', Liess went on. 'And they have fantastic composers – real geniuses.'
'Oh yes!' Ina replied smiling at her.
'How are you? Does it hurt?'
'A little', Ina admitted. 'But it's worse, when I close my eyes. Then I'm in that hall again and see Garos and the others in my mind…'
'Oh my dear', said Liess sighing, 'that's inevitable. First you'll have to learn to get over this horrible story, and

that takes its time.'

Ina looked silently into her wrinkled face.

'You must surmount yourself and talk about it, no matter to whom. That will help you to overcome your fears.' She paused for a moment and then she said cheerfully: 'Try my flower stew. You'll like it.'

Ina sat up cautiously and tried a bit. Oh, she was terribly hungry!

'It's wonderful', she said between two bits.

'I'm delighted', said Liess. 'When you finish your dinner, I have to see your ankles and wrists. These glowing fettles have burnt you badly, much more than your sister. It's clear that you tried to defend yourself.'

'Liess, I had no chance.' Ina sighed.

'I know.'

Ina closed her eyes. She was extremely tired. She hardly noticed Liess' treatment and didn't even wake up, when Maris entered the lab.

'Ina?' Maris asked cautiously and stroked softly Ina's hair. 'I'm sorry I couldn't come to Enu to help you.' Ina looked at the Sathorjan woman in amazement. 'I couldn't fly with the others because I had to look after my grandchildren. Shora, Nimi and Vons went on holiday for a couple of days – well, that's a grandmother's fate…'

Ina thought of her grandmother who had died much too early.

'Ina!' Maris became serious. 'I would like to apologize.'

'But why? It's not your fault', replied Ina without understanding.

'I didn't stop that experiment before although I could have done so', Maris explained with tears in her eyes.

'You wanted to save your daughter; that's reasonable', Ina replied.

'That's not a good reason to destroy somebody's life', Maris said unhappily.

'Maris, you didn't!'

'I almost did, my dear.'

'Maris, my life has changed completely, but it's wonderful.'
'What do you say? A couple of days ago they almost killed you!'
'Maris, I'm alive and I get the chance to become a Sathorjan. Moreover, I have Farres, my family and many friends.' Ina paused for a moment; then she went on: 'I'm happy I could keep my ability to breathe under water, you know? It means a lot to me.'
Maris couldn't believe her ears. She embraced the terrestrial girl exaltedly: 'Thank you very much, Ina', she whispered happily.
Ina was restless. Maris and Liess had left her more than an hour ago. They had promised they would tell Farres to come to see her. However, he hadn't come to the lab. Ina was missing her boyfriend, and she needed his help. At the moment she had no CC3. Her old device had disappeared, and she hadn't got a new one yet. Thus she couldn't communicate with anybody;
she had to wait. And that was exactly the problem: She needed someone who could bring her to the toilet.
A little later she swung her feet out of bed and stood up cautiously. Step by step she sneaked through the laboratory passing in between the machines. The longer she was out of her bed, the more she became aware of her physical weakness. When she came back from the toilette, she heard Farres furious voice. 'You have to do something about it!'
'I know', replied Ronok. 'I've already talked to Xio and Losos. However, I'm not sure if they'll renounce to perform that imbecilic confrontation.'
'But where is Ina?' Farres asked astonished. He looked around searching her. 'Darling!' he called out when he saw her beside one of the big ashlars. 'What are you doing there?'
'I had to go to…' She saw Ronok's facial expression and fell silent.

Farres took her onto his arms and brought her back to her bed.
'You should have called me', Ronok said annoyed. 'Walking around no matter how far is not good for your tormented body.'
Ina nodded. She was happy, when he returned to his devices without paying any more attention to her.
'What sort of confrontation is that?' Ina asked intrigued.
'You don't want to know', said Farres sighing. He took her hand and looked into her eyes.
'Darling, How are you?'
'More or less okay', Ina replied, 'I feel as if I were about fifty years older.' She smirked. Cautiously Farres embraced his girlfriend hugging her tenderly.
'I love you', he whispered into Ina's ear.
'I love you, too', replied the terrestrial girl.
She let herself slide back gently into the bed.
'Do you want to sleep now?' Farres asked his girlfriend compassionately.
'Soon', she sighed. 'I'm very tired. Everything is tremendously strenuous for me.'
'Let her rest', said Ronok. 'Anyway, there's little time left.'

Ina slept for an hour. Farres was sitting at her bed talking to Ronok in a low voice.
'Thank you very much for helping my father without any remuneration', said Farres.
'Zed could have contacted me long time ago', Ronok replied shaking his head. 'I suppose he has already been suffering these disorders for years, hasn't he?' Farres nodded.
Suddenly Sesa dashed into the laboratory shouting: 'Mom, Dad! Come in quickly.'
'Sesa!' Ronok cried furiously. 'You're not allowed to bring these terrestrials here!'
'Don't put on airs!' Chris nagged. 'You must allow us to visit our daughter!'

'Ina urgently needs to sleep and you just waked her up!' Ronok got annoyed.
'Well, we didn't know' Chris replied.
Ronok took a deep breath to calm down and then he said: 'If Ina wants, you can see her for a few minutes.'
Ina saw her mother's begging eyes and nodded. Elsa hugged Ina, kissed her on her brow, and whispered: 'Please don't let them take you away from us, too!'
'Mom, I'm an adult person', replied Ina. 'This adoption is the only way for me to lead a free, self-determined life.'
'Do you really want to belong to this bizarre conglomerate of people and be a citizen of the United Planets?' her father asked disdainfully. 'What else must happen, so that you understand you'll never really belong to them? You are from Earth; you have to accept this and come back to us!' Chris looked at her with annoyance.
'We could return to Earth with Sesa and you to start a new life', Elsa said while she tenderly stroked Ina's reddish blonde hair out of her face. Ina didn't like it, however, she allowed it. When she was a little girl she had enjoyed her mother's affectionate touch, but this was long ago.
'Mom, I can't go back there', she declared, 'nor do I want to.'
'What do you mean?' Chris asked enraged.
'With gills, Dad?' Ina shook her head angrily. 'Besides I have fallen in love and…'
'With that Sathorjan!' her father called out scornfully looking at Farres. 'On Earth you can find much better men.'
'Dad!' Ina said annoyed and tried to get up, but her boyfriend tenderly held her back. 'Never mind, darling!'
'Well, for heaven's sake then take him along with you!' Chris said sighing. 'Concerning your gills you can visit a cosmetic surgeon and have them removed.'
'Do you seriously think it's that easy? Do you know what will happen if somebody gets to know my secret? They'll think I'm an alien and…'

Ina fell silent, turned away and cried bitterly.
'Please, don't do that to her!' Farres shouted furiously and embraced Ina affectionately.
'What's the problem?' the terrestrial asked unnerved.
'She is dreadfully afraid', Ronok stated factually.
Maris rushed to the visitors and said most urgently: 'The chairman of the council will arrive here any moment with Xio; Losos and all the others. It's just a question of a few minutes.'
'You should go now', Ronok said to the terrestrial couple.
'Why? Just because that swellheaded wannabe president is coming?' Ina's father asked provocatively. 'I think we have a right to be there, when they are going to take away our daughter.'
'That's right. What else could they do to us?' Elsa asked.
'They could send you back into isolation', Ronok replied icily.
'Xio won't dare to', shouted Chris. 'Don't you think so, Sesa?'
'Daddy, I don't know', Sesa stammered timidly. She looked at her CC3 and said: 'Let's go!' But it already was too late.

Xio rushed into the laboratory accompanied by a tall, slender man with black eyes. His turquoise color cape gave him a majestic air. Losos and Nuna followed them a minute later.
Xio cast a brief look at the terrestrials, but didn't say anything.
'Are they Ina and Sesa's biological parents?' asked the stranger who introduced himself as Cho, the chairman of the council of delegates.
'Yes, they wished to visit my sister', Sesa stammered.
Well, we'll decide another day what will happen to them', Cho stated in a calm and quiet voice. 'If you wish, of course you can stay.'

Xio and Losos looked astonished at Cho. They hadn't thought he would be so generous. The chairman justly had the reputation of being fair and liberal. He didn't make any difference between citizens of the planetary community and inferior beings.
All of a sudden Sesa panicked screaming: 'No' and receding into the furthermost corner of the lab. Ina followed her sister's look and observed Zaq entering the lab accompanied by Tunia, the TFR.
'Why?' she asked. Her entire body was trembling. Zaq was the author of her appalling odyssey. Why did he have to come to the lab?
'Did you have to do that?' Ronok got annoyed. 'Didn't I ask you expressively to abstain from this confrontation? Both sisters have suffered enough due to him!'
Maris and Elsa had followed Sesa and tried to calm her down. Farres had embraced Ina protectively.
'I hope you know our legislation.' Losos cast an angry look at Ronok.
Cho, the chairman, took a quick glance at Ina and looked around in search of Sesa. Then his eyes wandered to Zaq who was standing with a brightly reddened face a few yards away from him. 'That was really unnecessary. Tunia, bring the prisoner back to his cell.'
'Pardon me', Losos said, 'that's our responsibility, nor yours.'
'No, it's the delegates competence', Cho replied coldly.
'And you can simply place yourself about our legislation preventing the confrontation?' Nuna asked confused.
'It's an exception. This absurd law needs a revision. I don't see the sense of confronting the victims of a crime with the perpetrator. Anyway, there's clear evidence indicating who the culprit is.'
'A wise man', Chris said appreciatively. 'These stupid laws her are really scraping the barrel!'
'Shut up!' Losos shouted wrathfully.

'Cho, couldn't you allow my wife and me to stay in the palace? I suppose you are familiar with our tragic history. We have been terribly wronged. If we have to lose Ina to the planetary community, at least we could stay in contact with her and Sesa.'
Cho looked at Chris thoughtfully.
'In your case I just have an advisory function. This issue has to be decided by the president and his wife.'
Chris stared at him furiously, but he didn't say a word.
'Well', said Cho turning to Ina who was lying pale faced and exhausted in her bed. Pain had started to torture her, and she was thirsty and weary.
Sesa had sat down to her sister on the bed holding her hand. Elsa stood beside her daughters. Lost in thoughts, she silently took a brief glance at Farres. Would he be good to Ina? Would their relation have a chance at all? Then she looked at Ina observing her lovingly. She had grown up and was a pretty young lady now. It almost broke her heart, when she thought about the deadly terror her elder daughter must have endured. And they even tried to sell her younger daughter! She shook her head when she imagined it. What a terrible world was that?
'Ina, in five days the procedure for the adoption will take place. You have to go punctually at nine in the morning to the small hearing room for the inquiry. The subsequent voting will decide, if the adoption is granted or not.'
Ina swallowed and looked at Cho with widened eyes.
'Each of the attendees has the right to ask you one or more questions. The delegates will ask what they consider important.' The chairman paused, thought for a while, and then he went on: 'Well the matter with Shora will bring your much closer to your goal. And the fact that you've been the only one to bring up the precious Gaia-fruits from the rift. The people entitled to vote will like that. I suppose you will keep offering your help.'
'Of course', Ina whispered.

'That's good. With your adoption you'll have all the citizen's rights, but all the duties, too. You'll have to learn many things and pursue a regular job.'
A job? What qualifications did she have? Everything she had learned on Earth, on Sathorja was useless or rather ridiculous.
'Xio will find something appropriate for you. Maybe your job will have to do with water', Cho explained with a wink.
'Which examinations does she have to take?' Sesa wanted to know.
'I don't know exactly, but the important subjects certainly will be politics, economics, and the planetary community's legislation. Furthermore, perhaps geography and especially for Ina limnology.'
Was he serious?
'And how much time will Ina have to learn all that stuff?' Farres asked intrigued.
'This will be announced. First we must wait and see the results of the hearing.'
Ina felt like at the beginning of a course of studies. She saw mountains of manuscripts in front of her mind's eye.
'That was all I had to tell you, Ina. We'll meet again in the hearing room. Have a rest. You need it badly!'
Ina nodded. She was happy, when everybody had left the laboratory. Finally she could sleep.

'Today is the great day', Sesa said radiant with joy when she entered the lab at half past eight.
Ina had fulfilled Ronok's request. She had stayed in bed and allowed him to care for her. That morning she was terribly nervous. She couldn't eat anything, ran up and down in the lab, and didn't listen to Maris' optimistic words.
She looked into the mirror straightening her hairdo.
'Don't tell me you're afraid of the hearing!' Sesa called out. 'You should be happy. Soon you'll be a Sathorjan. That's fantastic. At last you can do whatever you wish.'
'Frankly I don't know what's awaiting me. They are constantly talking about duties.'
'It won't be too bad. Look at me!'
'Your case is different. You have grown up and gone to school here', Ina said. 'How can I get that entire syllabus into my head?'
'Maybe learning it', Sesa said smirking.
Angrily Ina shook her head.
'Well, my dear girls', Maris started to say, 'in a few minutes you have to set out. By the way Ina, you should know the hearing will take place without spectators.'
'Yes, I know', Ina said full of melancholy.
'It'll go well. Don't worry. We'll keep our fingers crossed.'
'Ina, I'll be with you!' Sesa said consoling. 'They allowed me to be there to support you. Isn't that great?' Sesa took Ina's hand and pulled her up. Ina would have preferred to have Farres at her side.

'What do you think, Maris, is Ina looking good enough for the delegates?' Sesa asked enthusiastically.
'Oh yes!' Maris said smiling.
Ina was wearing a emerald green costume and matching shoes. The fancy dress had patterns of its own, but it was discreet. She had put up her long, dense, reddish blond hair. Sesa felt comfortable in her wine red two piece suit. It was a good match to her petite figure. Her chestnut brown hair fell over her shoulder and made her look even younger than she was.
'Well girls! You have to go. Good luck, Ina!'
'Thank you', replied the terrestrial.

A transporter brought the two girls to the small hearing room. The gates opened automatically, and Sesa lead Ina to the podium in the room's center. Cho, the chairman, nodded toward the sisters. Sesa went to a sofa opposite Ina who slowly lifted her gaze.
She was facing a wide variety of men and aliens. 'Breathe deeply and calm down', she said to herself. This exactly was very difficult for her as she was sitting there in the limelight.
The murmurs in the hall fell silent at once when Cho raised his voice.
'Today the case of the terrestrial Ina will be negotiated. Everybody is familiar with the issue; the corresponding documents have been distributed.'
An increasing whispering was in the air.
'So let's start! Ina is at your disposal for any question you might want to ask her. She will answer to the best of her knowledge.'
'Why do you want to become a Sathorjan?' a corpulent woman asked. She had a pale face with lilac eyes; her lilac hair was stringy and unkempt – at least for Ina.
Ina issued her statements carefully, nevertheless she was asked to speak loudly and clearly.
'Are you grateful for being here?'

'Yes', Ina stammered.
'Why?' She numerated all the advantages of her life on Sathorja.
'In the beginning you wished to return to your planet Earth, didn't you?'
'Yes, but that was long time ago.'
'How's your relationship to your parents?' a creature with red scales in the second row asked her.
'First I have to get used to their retrieval.' – And how is your relationship to Bora and Xio?'
'I respect them', Ina murmured timidly. So far she hadn't reflected about the meaning of being adopted by the two.
'Did you reconcile with Ronok or will you sue him for the experiment when you are a Sathorjan?'
For a moment Ina fell silent; then she said quickly: 'I won't undertake persecution against him.'
'Do you think you can live here like a freeloader?' somebody asked.
'No!' Ina replied perplexed. 'I want to work for my living such as everybody else does.'
'Diving? Do you call that work?'
Ina's face was getting hot, quite the contrary to her hands. They were cold and wet holding on to each other.
'Are you planning to go on bewitching other women's men?' a woman asked furiously.
Ina didn't know what to say. The unfairness of that question was obvious, wasn't it?
'Glynia?' the chairman asked. 'Are you here on behalf of Rida's parents? Don't you know that they have committed punishable offences?'
The hall grew louder.
'They are subject of a criminal investigation, so you better keep your mouth shut', Cho went on calmly.
'They haven't done any wrong. But this terrestrial beast has. Everybody knows that Farres was Rida's boyfriend and…'

'That doesn't matter for the subject of this hearing, Glynia. Furthermore, everybody in the room apart from you knows that Ina cannot be blamed for Rida's misery. However we are quite certain that Rida's parents have sponsored Zaq to eliminate Ina. Soon we shall obtain the necessary evidence. Money transfers can always be traced back, because they are subject to strictest guidelines.'
'No!' Glynia gasped, sank back into her seat, and fell silent.
'Silence please!' shouted the chairman into the rising murmurs. 'Forget the last questions! They are irrelevant and have nothing to do with the subject of this hearing.'
The next question came immediately: 'Will you stay with Farres?' a young woman asked from far behind. Ina's cheeks were glowing when she nodded. 'I love him' she whispered.
'Why did you save Shora?' an egg yolk yellow, hairy creature asked staring at her with his three eyes.
'I couldn't stand to see her suffer', the terrestrial stammered shyly.
'Do you suffer from anxiety states?'
Ina nodded timidly.
'Will you continue to dive for healing fruits?'
'Yes!' Ina said clearly.
After a longer pause Cho looked around and asked: 'Can we vote now?'
'Yes', most of the attendees called.
Ina wanted to stand up and leave the room.
'No, you can wait here. We just need a minute', the chairman said.
In fact, shortly afterwards Cho called out the result: 'Ina becomes a citizen of the United Planets. The adoption has been approved. Her adoptive parents are Xio, our president and his wife Bora.'
Ina could hardly believe it. Sesa flung her arms around her neck and whispered: 'Congratulations!'

The gates opened and people streamed into the hall, first and foremost Farres. He took Ina into his arms and pressed her up against him. 'Darling!' he called out enthusiastically. 'You did it! Now you are one of us.'
Ina couldn't believe it. Around her a chaos had broken out; she had to shake lots of hands, paws, and claws.
'How can everybody know about it?' she asked her boyfriend in hushed whispers.
'Your success has been spreading like a wildfire', Farres said smirking. He stood behind her creating a free space, so the enthusiastic crow couldn't trample her to death.

An hour later Farres brought her back to the laboratory.
'Darling, do I really have to go back?' Ina asked unwillingly.
'You don't have to', the young man replied. 'But I want to go out with you for a special dinner tonight, hence you must be fit.'
Ina looked at him in surprise.
'We have much to celebrate!' Farres grinned. 'So you better have a little rest. Ronok told me, last night you didn't sleep at all.'
Ina nodded and went back to bed. She was happy and unburdened, but also tremendously weary. When would she finally feel fit again? Many things went through her mind that day.
How would her life go on? As a Sathorjan from that moment on she had the same rights as all the other people and creatures. Rida had no chance to bully her around anymore. Her parents even had to be prepared for a punishment.
Ina reached for her glass and suddenly hesitated. What had happened to Garos and his red eyed girlfriend Lysi? Where were they? On Enu? 'Never mind', Ina thought. From that moment on she was under the protection of the community of the planets. This was incredible. Ina took a deep breath enjoying the feeling of unlimited freedom.

When Ina was sitting in the underwater restaurant with Farres that evening, she still thought she was dreaming. She found it very hard to accept that she had won.
'Is it really true?' she asked.
'Yes darling. You have recovered your family, and you won another one. You have me on your neck, my brother, sister, my parents, and many friends. Yes, you are a Sathorjan. You have hit the jackpot!'
Farres took Ina's hand into his hand and caressed it tenderly.
'We have always known it', Ina heard a voice inside her head. She looked around observing the water behind the glass walls. A herd of Iaos had gathered in front of the glass panel looking at her with their beautiful eyes.
'You have made friends.'
'Yes, I have, and much more', she replied in thoughts.

Acknowledgments

I would like to give my special thanks to Margot, Marelise, Brigitte, Peta P., and Petra B. who read my manuscript in advance inspiring me with their ideas and suggestions for improvement. I also want to thank Christian who made it possible for me to materialize this book project.